"So what is th...
going to entai...

"Ever shoot a gun or wire a bomb?" Brady asked.

"No and no."

"Kill someone?"

"No!"

"Well, then," he said lightly. "We've got our work cut out for us."

"You want me to kill someone?" Eve gasped. "I'd never kill anyone. Not for you. Not for anyone!"

"Never say never, Miss Dupont."

"Call me Eve."

"If you'll call me Brady. We're going to be working very closely for the next few months. We might as well dispense with the formalities."

"Why didn't you ask if I'd kill you if I had a gun?" she asked sweetly.

So much for a truce. He snorted. "I already know the answer to that one," he answered grimly.

★ ★ ★

"Like" us on Facebook at
www.facebook.com/RomanticSuspenseBooks
and check us out on www.eHarlequin.com!

Dear Reader,

I don't know about you, but I've been waiting a *long* time for Brady Hathaway to finally find the right woman. He first showed up in my Medusa series several years ago and stubbornly remained a bachelor for my next half dozen books. I was beginning to despair of him ever finding true love.

Thankfully, Eve Dupont came along to give him everything he could handle and more. The magnificent beauty of the French Pyrenees Mountains is the perfect place to shape a woman of the strength and fire necessary to land a man like Brady, and American-born Eve is no exception.

Some stories are just so much fun to write it hardly seems fair to call it work, and this was one of them for me. Every day, I sat down at my computer eager to see what these two characters would cook up next to tempt and tease each other. And I have to say, they rarely let me down. I sincerely hope you have at least half as much fun watching their love story unfold as I did.

So put on your favorite beach wear, pour yourself a tall glass of something cold and refreshing, and come on down to the sunny Caribbean to watch Brady put up one valiant (and losing) last stand against the woman of his dreams.

All my best,

Cindy Dees

CINDY DEES

Soldier's Last Stand

ROMANTIC
SUSPENSE

Recycling programs
for this product may
not exist in your area.

ISBN-13: 978-0-373-27735-3

SOLDIER'S LAST STAND

Copyright © 2011 by Cynthia Dees

www.Harlequin.com

Printed in U.S.A.

Books by Cindy Dees

CINDY DEES

started flying airplanes while sitting in her dad's lap at the age of three and got a pilot's license before she got a driver's license. At age fifteen, she dropped out of high school and left the horse farm in Michigan where she grew up to attend the University of Michigan. After earning a degree in Russian and East European Studies, she joined the U.S. Air Force and became the youngest female pilot in its history. She flew supersonic jets, VIP airlift and the C-5 Galaxy, the world's largest airplane. During her military career, she traveled to forty countries on five continents, was detained by the KGB and East German secret police, got shot at, flew in the first Gulf War and amassed a lifetime's worth of war stories. Her hobbies include medieval reenacting, professional Middle Eastern dancing and Japanese gardening.

This RITA® Award-winning author's first book was published in 2002 and since then she has published more than twenty-five bestselling and award-winning novels. She loves to hear from readers and can be contacted at www.cindydees.com.

This book is for my great-aunt Ginny,
who faithfully reads every book I write,
and for my cousins Eric and Keith. If there is such a
thing as a storytelling gene, mine surely comes from
this branch of my family. Thanks for the stories and
laughter around your kitchen table that taught me
everything I know about spinning a fine tale.

Chapter 1

The moment the alarms went off in the cavernous twilight of the H.O.T. Watch Ops Center, a map of the Western Hemisphere flashed up on one of the three jumbo screens mounted high on the wall of the massive room. A red, electronic sunburst blinked ominously over Kingston, Jamaica, indicating that surveillance satellites had picked up an explosion.

"Say size and location of detonation," Navy Commander Brady Hathaway barked across the loud speakers into the tense silence.

One of the intelligence analysts on the floor replied tersely, "Knutsford Boulevard, Kingston. Looks like the Dred-Naught Dance Club. Initial estimate is upward of twenty sticks worth of TNT."

Brady sucked in his breath. That was a freaking big explosion. "Capacity of that club?" he asked.

Another tech replied in his headset, "Coming up now, sir."

A pause. "Fire code says six hundred. But knowing Jamaica, more like a thousand would be in there on a Saturday night at the height of the tourist season."

"Get me visual," he ordered, although no doubt the highly trained satellite technicians on the floor were already on that obvious next step.

"Visual from S-105 in thirty-four seconds," someone announced over the loudspeakers.

"Visual from S-22 in ninety-six seconds," another tech announced.

Not bad. Two satellites engaged in under two minutes. And S-105 carried the latest in high-tech digital cameras. If the bomber had stuck around to watch his work, H.O.T. Watch might just grab a facial image of the guy on their telemetry.

Although Kingston had its share of political turbulence, it wasn't one of the outright violent corners of the Caribbean. Likely there'd been a bunch of Americans in the club, though. And that meant U.S. government officials galore were about to breathe fire down his neck to produce an ID on the bomber.

It was going to be a long night.

Some hours later—it was hard to feel time passing in the underground facility—someone called his name. Brady looked up from his workstation on the edge of the floor and spied his civilian counterpart, Jennifer Blackfoot, gesturing to him to join her. The tall, slender Native American's dark eyes looked worried. He jogged up the metal stairs to join her on the observation deck looking out over the rows of technicians and analysts.

"What's up?" he asked without preamble. They'd worked together for nearly seven years and didn't need many words to communicate effectively.

"We got a facial hit," she replied.

"Good work." Wow. That was fast. There had been hundreds

of faces outside the nightclub when the bomb blew, and thousands milling around the area within moments afterward.

She jerked her head to indicate they should step into the soundproof briefing room behind them. He followed her inside and the door sealed, making his ears pop lightly.

"Who did you spot?" he asked.

"A woman. Annika Cantori."

He frowned. "That name rings a bell."

Jennifer prompted, "Cruise ship hijacking five years ago. You sent in the Medusas to liberate the ship."

The memory clicked. A team of terrorists had taken over the cruise ship *Grand Adventure* and offloaded all the male crew and passengers, leaving behind only women and children. The Medusas—an all-female Special Forces team— had infiltrated the ship and ultimately killed the terrorists and freed the vessel. However, the Medusas had always been convinced they'd missed a female terrorist who'd been planted among the passengers to pass information to her male comrades.

After the hijacking, H.O.T. Watch had done an exhaustive analysis of the passengers and identified a woman named Annika Cantori as the likely female terrorist. She was one of the only passengers never to file an insurance claim against the cruise ship company, and she'd completely disappeared immediately after the hijacking, not to be seen or heard from since. H.O.T. Watch had performed multiple searches of credit card, banking, traffic, voter registration and even library data bases the world over looking for Annika, to no avail. She'd gone completely off the grid. Very suspicious, indeed.

His colleague flashed up a grainy picture of a woman on the white wall at the end of the room. As he watched, the picture refreshed itself several times, each time coming more sharply into focus as photo enhancement software did its magic on the image. Finally, a picture of a lean, hard-looking woman came into focus. Jennifer announced, "This image came from across the street from the Dred-Naught approximately fifty seconds before the bombing."

Another picture flashed up on the wall beside the first one of a woman in perhaps her late twenties. This photo was at a range of about twelve feet and unmistakable. "This one comes from our database of passengers on the Grand Adventure."

"The facial recognition program has made a positive ID. These two images are the same woman. Annika Cantori. Our mysteriously disappeared ship passenger."

"But now she's back?" Brady guessed.

"Apparently."

"What did she do after the nightclub explosion?"

"She stayed. Watched the emergency response. Possibly was hanging around to get a preliminary body count for herself."

"Ballsy," he commented.

"It gets better," Jennifer replied grimly. "She hasn't even bothered to flee the Caribbean. She hopped a flight this morning to Grand Cayman Island."

"You think she's going to take a nice vacation on the beach to celebrate her success?" Brady asked skeptically.

"Doubtful. She strikes me as the type who'll keep going until someone catches her, or at least scares the bejeezus out of her and forces her back into hiding for a few years."

If Jennifer was right, this woman had to be stopped, and the sooner the better. Before she killed any more innocents. "How do you want to proceed?" Brady asked soberly.

"We need to get proof that she's the bomber. Find out what she's up to in the Caymans. I hesitate to try passive surveillance on her, though. I think she'd spot it. I'm thinking an infiltration of her cell is the way to go."

"Tricky business to run an infiltration on someone like her.

She's got to be as paranoid as hell. And based on last night, she's organized and intelligent. She'd smell an undercover man a mile away."

Jennifer smiled, although the expression owed more to wolflike aggression than good humor. "That's why I'm sending in a woman."

Logical. The Medusas were highly experienced operators and would leap at a chance to catch the fish who'd gotten away before. Still, they were military. "Annika may spot a Medusa, too. Particularly since she knows female Special Forces types exist in our military."

"And that would be why I'm not sending in a Medusa," she replied. A new photograph flashed up on the wall.

Brady jolted as the most beautiful woman he'd seen in years threw him a sultry smile guaranteed to melt any man's shorts. The phrase "flesh impact" came to mind. Beauty queen. Knockout. Kowabunga. "Whoa. Who's that?" he blurted.

"Eve Dupont. Her brother, Viktor, led the terrorist team that hijacked the *Grand Adventure.* I want to use her to get inside Annika's cell."

He frowned. "Does she have any training? How do you know she doesn't share her brother's rather extreme political views? Do you know if she'd even help us?"

"That's where you come in," Jennifer replied cryptically.

Huh? He wasn't even close to the right person to be involved with infiltrating a hard-core terrorist group. He looked military, he acted military and, frankly, impersonating a cold, calculating killer had never been his greatest strength as a field operator. Not to mention he didn't often go out on missions anymore. Every now and then he went out to supervise a particularly tricky operation, but he mostly left the heroics to the younger men and women in his special operations teams. At thirty-nine, he was starting to feel the long years of hard demands on his body.

He glanced back at the picture of Eve wearing only a skimpy bikini and a tan. Her legs were a mile long, and although she was slender, she filled out her bikini top impressively in open defiance of gravity. Her eyes were some pale color that glowed in contrast to her bronze skin, and her mane of wavy golden hair framed a face so stunningly beautiful his heart skipped a beat.

"She's some looker," he remarked lightly.

"Hence, my bringing this one to you. I don't have any male operatives I trust to work with this woman and not try to bed her. But you—" Jennifer broke off.

Not liking where her logic was headed, Brady scowled. "But I *what?*" he demanded.

She shrugged. "I've never once seen a woman turn your head. As far as I can tell you're immune to them."

He snorted. Hardly. He just flatly refused to mix business and pleasure. And since his business was pretty much a 24/7 job, that left no time for female entanglements in his life. Not to mention he didn't have much use for civilian women in general, and his female colleagues were off-limits.

"Gee. Thanks," he retorted wryly. At least Jennifer hadn't openly accused him of being gay.

She challenged, "You tell me which one of your guys you'd turn loose to handle a woman who looks like that. And whom you wouldn't be scared to death of losing his head over her."

He sighed. "I see your point."

"You're the only man in this facility I'd trust to handle her."

Hell, he had no trouble at all imagining handling all that glamour-goddess perfection, those silky legs wrapped around him, his hands filled to overflowing with her bountiful—

Yeah. He definitely saw Jenn's point. He might not trust

women, but he didn't trust a bunch of horny male operatives, either.

He spoke past a suddenly dry throat, "So, you want to use her to infiltrate Annika's cell. And do what once you're in?"

"Find out if Annika was behind the Dred-Naught bombing and, more importantly, what she's planning next. Then stop it."

He leaned back skeptically. "This Dupont girl's an amateur. Why not try one of the Medusas? They're experienced and do undercover work all the time."

She replied, "I spoke with their commander, Vanessa Blake. Both of her teams are on jobs. As interested as she was in pulling one of her operatives in to do this mission, she can't spare anyone right now." Jennifer leaned forward in her seat. "Besides, I think you're exactly right. Annika would spot any kind of trained operative in a heartbeat. It's why I'm not even bothering to suggest pulling in a CIA agent. Better that we send in a legitimate amateur who makes no claims to being anything else."

It made a certain sense. "You'd be putting Eve at terrible risk. And how certain are you she'd cooperate with us anyway? For all we know she sympathizes with her big—and may I remind you, dead—brother's politics. She may think Viktor was some kind of hero who died a martyr to the cause. If we recruit her, she could turn on us at the worst possible moment. She could blow not only the mission but the cover of whoever's handling her."

Jennifer's one word response made his blood run cold. "Exactly."

She knew him too well. He'd never send one of his men out on a suicide mission. If anyone was going to tangle with lovely Eve Dupont, he'd choose himself for the job.

He glanced at the picture of the young woman on the wall. Eve laughed back at him like some kind of sea goddess. A still-life siren calling to him. Would she try to steal away his will and enslave him as the original Sirens had done to the unfortunate sailors who listened to their songs? His gaze hardened. She could try. But he wasn't kidding. He didn't get involved with women. Ever.

Eve Dupont climbed the steps from the relatively dry, warm London tube station into a cold, gray November drizzle. She couldn't believe they'd insisted she meet yet another government man, particularly on a nasty day like this.

How many times was she going to have to tell these jokers she didn't know anything? She'd never been a terrorist herself, she'd never had any clue Viktor was a terrorist, and she'd never seen or heard anything on his visits home to indicate what he was planning or who he worked with.

The restaurant where she was supposed to meet this latest investigator came into view. It looked like a classy place, frankly a lot nicer than she'd expected. At least she was going to get a decent free lunch out of it. That was an improvement over the last pair of Interpol types who'd dragged her to their offices to interrogate her like a common criminal.

She ducked into the dim interior of the restaurant. The lunch rush had mostly cleared out, but everyone still in the place turned to stare as she shed her raincoat. She sighed, used to the reaction. Even when she wore a chunky sweater and sloppy jeans they stared at her. She could probably wear a burlap sack and they'd still gape.

It wasn't that she hated being beautiful. She just wished people saw more than some beddable blonde. She supposed most women would bitch-slap her for whining about her looks, and maybe they were right. Maybe she should just enjoy her beauty while she had it.

A tall, dark-haired man stood up from a table in the corner

and advanced toward her. He had to be her date. The short hair, stern jaw and direct stare were a dead giveaway.

Sure enough, he murmured, "Miss Dupont. I'm Brady Hathaway. It's nice to meet you." He held out a big, calloused, *tanned* hand. Where did anyone get a tan in this part of the world at this time of year? She'd give her eyeteeth to be on a hot beach somewhere, soaking up some rays.

And then his accent registered. American, huh? She didn't tell people often that she held a dual American-French citizenship. Her mother had been American, and she'd been born in the States. But she mostly considered herself to be French. Her countrymen hadn't tortured her in a while. What did they want with her now? She ignored his big, powerful-looking hand and looked him square in his steel-gray eyes. "Let's get this over with, shall we?"

He looked momentarily taken aback, but nodded evenly enough. "As you like. This way."

Those Americans did grow their men big and muscular. She was struck by how he towered over her, and she was no shorty herself, standing almost five-foot-nine. He guided her to his table, which was predictably tucked into a dark corner with no other patrons nearby. He held her chair for her. She almost registered it as a kindness before recalling he was yet another official type who wanted something from her.

It didn't take a rocket scientist to spot his wingmen. They were seated on the other side of the restaurant with perfect sight lines to her and all the exits. Based on the bad suits and worse haircuts, she'd guess they were MI6. Low-level administrative types pulled off desk jobs to babysit the visiting American.

"Can I get you a drink?" the visiting American asked politely enough.

"Sure," she drawled. "Gin and tonic." The poison of choice in her family. It had put *Maman* six feet under. Eve stared into the drink when it arrived. Was she headed down the same road? Would she grow bitter and cynical at life's disappointments and give up someday like her mother? She took a sip of the drink, savoring its sharp bite. Heck, she already had the cynical part wired.

"Thank you for agreeing to speak with me," her companion said in a pleasant rumble.

Like she had any choice? The first time she refused to cooperate with one of these government bureaucrats was the moment she got put on every terrorist watch list in the world. She could forget ever going through an airport in peace again or getting a visa for, oh, anywhere. Not to mention this sort of harassment would increase exponentially in frequency and severity.

She dipped a manicured fingernail in her drink and stirred the ice cubes around idly. She pulled her finger out and sucked it seductively as she glanced up at him out of the corner of her eye. It might be mean to intentionally throw her questioner off balance by flirting with him, but she was sick to death of being hassled.

Usually the ploy worked like a charm, but Brady Hathaway did the strangest thing. He leaned back in his chair and studied her as if she were a mildly interesting insect. "Does that come-hither crap work on most men?"

Shock poured through her. He wasn't interested in her sexually? She didn't know whether to be insulted or profoundly relieved. She settled for scowling. "I have no idea what you're talking about."

"You don't lie very well. We would have to work on that."

He wanted her to lie? Huh?

Intelligence glinted in his piercing gaze. "Look. I'm not here to talk about what your deceased brother may or may not have done or to argue the relative merit or insanity of his political views. I'm here to talk about you."

Well, now. This was a new approach. Interested, she waited to see where he took the line of questioning.

He glanced over at his British minders and lowered his voice, "I've been sent here to ask for your help. But I happen to think it's a terrible idea and that you would fail spectacularly. I have no intention of letting you harm me or my men in the process."

Stung that he'd automatically assume she was a screwup, she demanded, "Why are you so sure I'd fail?"

He shrugged. "You strike me as the kind of woman who knows exactly the power of her looks and won't hesitate to use them…"

How dare he? That was so not true!

"…I need a woman of substance and strength for my mission. With courage and smarts and guts…"

Hey! She had all those things!

"…confess I was ordered to speak to you. I'm afraid this has been a waste of your time and mine, Miss Dupont. I will be happy to pay for your meal, of course."

She stared at him, genuinely shocked. "That's an impressive set of snap judgments you've made about me, Mr. Hathaway."

"I did my homework on you. I'm not wrong," he replied bluntly.

At a loss, she finally blurted, "So you're seriously not here to quiz me about my brother?"

One corner of his mouth turned up in a sardonic smile. "There's nothing you could tell me about his final years that I don't already know."

Indignation at getting brushed off like this flared in her gut. "Oh, so you think I've taken up the family business where he left off? Are you going to put a tracking burr on my clothes and follow me to see if I meet with any known terrorists in the next few weeks? I should warn you that I burn my clothes after these sorts of meetings along with tossing my cell phone and getting a new number."

He made a sound of approval. "If you didn't look like you do, I might say there's some hope for you. But as it is…" he trailed off regretfully.

Her looks were *preventing* him from giving her a shot at his mission? That was a first. The waiter came to take their order and she chose the most expensive dish on the menu— imported fresh lobster tails.

Their food came and she picked at it unenthusiastically. An emotion that took her a moment to identify coursed through her. Why was she feeling despair? Maybe because she was so bloody tired of living under the stigma of her brother's illegal activities, so tired of carrying the burden around. Why couldn't anyone just cut her a break? Give her one lousy chance to prove that she wasn't like Viktor.

"What's this mission of yours?" she demanded belligerently, praying her tone would disguise the ache in her soul.

He shrugged. "It's classified. I can't talk about it with you."

A little voice in the back of her head yelled that he was playing her. He was blatantly manipulating her into accepting whatever he was about to offer. But something in her gut wanted to play ball with this man. The very fact that he wasn't stumbling all over himself trying to figure out how to ask her out on a date was intriguing.

Frustrated, she asked, "Then why did you invite me to lunch?"

"I told you. I'm following orders. My superiors insisted I meet with you, in spite of my objections. They want me to verify that I pegged you correctly from your dossier." A pause, and then he added, "And I did."

He had a dossier on her? He was the first of his kind to openly admit it. She leaned forward and made deep eye contact with him. "And what did you decide from my dossier?"

His gaze, locked on hers, didn't waiver, not even for an instant. "You're too sure of yourself. You wouldn't take the work seriously. You're impulsive. Unpredictable and possibly unstable. You wouldn't do at all."

"You can stop with the reverse psychology, Mr. Hathaway. I have no interest whatsoever in helping any government with any mission."

He took a sip of the Guinness stout sitting before him and said grimly, "Then we are in agreement. We'll sit here and eat our lunch, and afterward we'll each return to our regularly scheduled lives."

"Agreed," she replied tightly. But something disappointed twisted in her gut. She'd always been such a compulsive overachiever. She hated walking away from a challenge. A psychologist would probably say she was compensating for her brother's spectacular failures. The psychologist would probably be right, too.

She sighed. When would she learn? Nothing she or anyone else could do would make Viktor's mistakes right. He'd harmed, even killed, dozens of people while chasing a ridiculous notion that the little guy could make a real difference. He had been desperate to be a major player on the world stage. But he'd failed to understand that heroes die young…and usually painfully.

No matter what heroic impulses pulsed in her veins, she was no dummy. She'd learned from big brother's premature demise. No way was she going to play hero for the man seated across the table from her.

"So. Tell me about your job," he said casually.

"We're going to make small talk?" she asked incredulously.

"Indulge me. This way the men watching me will report

to my superiors that I made a good-faith effort to talk you into doing the mission."

She might have refused him out of general principles, but then he flashed her a smile so sexy it totally derailed her train of thought. She mumbled, "I'm currently working as an artist for a major advertising firm. It's not a great job, but it's a job."

"Is it better or worse than sketching tourists on Montmartre for a few bucks a picture?" he asked.

He knew about that? She hadn't lived a hand-to-mouth hippie's life in Paris for years. "That's a good dossier you've got on me, Mr. Hathaway."

He shrugged in response. "You should see the one I've got on your brother."

"What would surprise me in his dossier?"

He studied her for long enough that she didn't think he was going to answer. But then he said, "Would it surprise you to know our profilers think your brother didn't believe the majority of the political drivel he spouted...and ultimately died for?"

The comment confirmed what she'd suspected for years. Hearing it from an expert on her brother lifted a weight off her shoulders she hadn't even known was there it until it went away.

"Thank you," she said quietly.

"For what?"

She didn't particularly care to explain herself to this man she would never see again. She shrugged. "Just thank you."

He gazed at her as if he knew exactly what she was thanking him for. "You're welcome."

"What else did the dossier say about him?" she asked.

"It said he was mostly responsible for raising you."

She frowned. "Did it now?"

"Is that true?" Hathaway asked.

Was it? She wasn't sure anyone had actually raised her. Their mother had always been a heavy drinker. Apparently, the practical reality of being swept off her feet by a romantic French tourist and uprooting her entire life to a different continent had been too much for her mother. The four of them had lived on a small pension her father had earned from serving in the French military. When he'd died, the pension benefit had decreased, along with their already poor standard of living. Viktor had spent most of his youth hustling the tourists who flocked to the French Pyrenees. He'd used the English their mother insisted on teaching them to take advantage of the unwary. And she—she'd just tried to get by. It had been a daily struggle to find food, get clothes to fit her ever growing frame, and to deal with her mother's increasingly erratic and violent behavior.

Eve blinked. Hathaway was studying her intently, his gray eyes clearly seeing far more than she'd like. She answered slowly, "It's more accurate to say that Viktor and I raised ourselves. Yes, he was older, but he had his own problems to deal with."

"Like abandonment issues with his mother and lack of a parental role model in his life?"

This stranger was cutting far too close to the quick for her taste. She snapped, "What right do you have to comment on our lives? You weren't there. You have no idea what we went through."

His gaze went dark. Closed. "Everyone has issues to deal with growing up. You're not unique in that."

She leaped on the opening he'd given her with all the predatory intensity of a shark on the hunt. "What issues did *you* have to deal with?"

He didn't answer right away and she glared at him. How dare he sit there, all perfect and sure of himself, safe in his superiority, hiding behind being in charge of this interview and so quick to judge her?

"Your mother was one kind of a nightmare. But there are plenty of other flavors of maternal failure."

Her eyebrows lifted. This self-assured man had a crappy mother, too? "Tell me about her," she replied.

He shrugged. "Old history. And we're not here to talk about me. We're here to talk about you."

"No, we're not. We're here to pretend to talk about me."

He nodded, conceding the point. "How long have you lived in London?"

"I suspect you already know the answer to that one. Is this a test?"

"Just making small talk, Miss Dupont."

"Five years. Ever since your soldiers killed my brother."

Hathaway retorted, "He signed his own death warrant when he hijacked that cruise ship. Do you think he was suicidal or merely deluded by his girlfriend? Our profilers debate the issue among themselves."

She leaned back, startled by the bluntness of the question. "Maybe a little of both. I wasn't there, so I don't know."

"That's my take on it, too. I think he knew he was in too deep with a woman and had no other recourse. Maybe he was trying to escape his entanglement with Annika Cantori and figured death was his only way out."

From what she remembered of Annika, that was entirely possible. Her mother had always believed the female terrorist was responsible for Viktor's death. But then, her mother spouted all kinds of crazy ideas when the gin was talking.

Hathaway was speaking again. "Either way, I'm sorry for your loss. Regardless of his politics or his stupid decisions, I know your brother meant a lot to you."

She stared at him, genuinely stunned. In all these years, he was the first official to express real sympathy over Viktor's death.

Hathaway turned his attention to his steak after that and they finished the meal in companionable silence. He made no effort to look down her sweater, nor did he make any offensive propositions to her, for which she was immensely grateful. And the man was not hard on the eye. Under other circumstances, she might have been interested in this too-perceptive American.

The check came, and he broke the silence with, "I'm sorry to have disrupted your day."

"You're seriously not going to ask me to help you in any way?" she blurted.

He looked at her steadily. "I'm seriously not."

"Are you really so sure I'd fail?" she couldn't resist pressing.

"You're not tough enough to see it through. You would most likely die, and I or one of my men would get hurt. I'm not willing to risk my men on you."

She stood up, offended that he cared more about putting his men in danger than her dying. Out of the corner of her eye, she noted that the MI6 men lurched in response to her abrupt movement.

"You don't know anything about me, Mr. Hathaway. You're wrong about me on several levels. I would wish you luck with your mission, but honestly, I hope you fail. And by the way, tell your minders to roll their tongues up and tuck them back in their mouths. I'm way out of their league."

She turned to storm out but was not fast enough to miss the flare of amusement in the American's dark eyes. Jerk.

Brady watched Eve Dupont sail out of the restaurant with all the drama of a movie star. Her rear end twitched angrily, and she gave one last toss of her hair as she disappeared from sight. A force of nature that woman was.

The two MI6 men joined him at his table. "Strike out, did you?" one of them asked sympathetically.

Brady smiled up at his hosts. "Not at all, gentlemen. It went swimmingly well, in fact."

"But she said no," the younger agent blurted.

"All in good time," Brady replied serenely. "She wanted to say yes, and that's all I needed to know. I hate to impose on you, chaps, but there's one more thing I need you to do for me...."

Eve napped on and off as the Gulfstream jet chased the setting sun across the Atlantic Ocean. As the plane descended, twilight turned the thickly forested island beneath her into a mound of violets and grays. The pilots wouldn't say anything more than her destination was a private island somewhere in the Caribbean.

The plane bumped onto the runway and taxied to a stop. The engines shut down and one of the pilots offloaded her luggage while the other one opened up a garagelike building and drove an electric golf cart out into the deepening dusk.

"You want us to take you up to the house, Miss Dupont?" one of them asked.

"Where is this house?"

"Top of the mountain. That track over there takes you to its front door."

"Actually, I'd rather head up alone if you don't mind," she replied. She wasn't crazy about having an audience for the big I-told-you-so from Brady Hathaway when she showed up unannounced on his front porch.

Damn MI6, anyway. She still couldn't believe they'd threatened to revoke her visa and detain her as a suspected terrorist unless she agreed to work with the skeptical

American. She'd tried to explain that he'd refused to work with her, but the Brits had completely ignored her, arranged a leave of absence from her job and given her a choice. Jail or a jet bound for Brady Hathaway.

She wasn't entirely furious that the Brits had forced her into this trip. The meeting with the American had gnawed at her. Not only did she resent his intrusive questions about her upbringing, but his accusations that she was unstable and incapable of seeing a project through grated on her nerves.

And then there was the bit about her using her looks to get what she wanted. The more she thought about that little observation, the hotter it made her. Truth be told, MI6 hadn't had to twist her arm too hard before she'd agreed to let them fly her out here.

She took a deep breath and slid behind the wheel of the golf cart. She had a few things to say to Brady Hathaway. And she *really* wasn't doing his mission, now.

"Do you need anything else, ma'am?" one of the pilots asked her.

"No, thanks."

The men headed for their jet. They'd explained earlier that their orders were to deliver her to Hathaway and then leave immediately. As she guided the cart onto the narrow path, the plane's engines cranked up behind her.

She briefly considered making for the jungle, but the night sounds emerging from it dissuaded her from going Robinson Crusoe—particularly since she had no idea whatsoever how to take care of herself in the wild. Give her a man-shark infested nightclub, and she was a pro at navigating the dangerous waters. But forests and bugs and wild creatures? Not so much.

The day's sultry heat was giving way to a pleasant tropical

warmth as the path climbed the mountainside. She thought she glimpsed a light up ahead, and her heart raced. Time to face the music—and the monster.

Chapter 2

Brady had just stepped out of the shower when he heard the airplane land. He smiled grimly as he toweled himself dry. Time for round two in his sparring match with Eve Dupont. He wondered if she'd figured out yet that he'd won the first round. Not only was she here, but she didn't think he'd forced her into it. A win-win for him. As her handler going forward, he would need her to see him as an ally, not the enemy.

He pulled on jeans and a black polo shirt and slipped outside. Might as well establish up front who was in charge around here. He slipped into the shadows as easily as breathing and settled in to wait for her.

It didn't take long for a golf cart to come into sight as the scream of jet engines rose and winking lights climbed into the black sky overhead. Planning to face him solo, was she? Gutsy girl. He'd have to disabuse her of the notion that she could manage him like all the other men she'd known.

She stopped in front of the veranda stretching across the

entire front of the single-story house. Stripes of light shone through the plantation shutters onto her long, silky legs as she swung out of the cart.

His gut tightened as he saw the barely there sundress she wore. Its halter top was held up by little more than a shoelace around her neck, and its hem skimmed the tops of her thighs. The woman oozed pure sex. His instinct to take control of this encounter had been spot on.

He glided out of his hiding place as she climbed the shallow front steps and approached the door. He waited until she reached up to knock and then pounced, shoving her face-first into the wooden panel of the front door.

She let out a startled scream.

"What the hell are you doing here?" he growled. He registered the long, lush lines of her body pressing against his. Irritated, he beat down his visceral reaction to the feel of her. He was *not* some rookie to lose himself in lust.

She relaxed between him and the door. "Brady?" she purred throatily.

The sound of her voice was thick and sweet like warm honey dripping over him. "Answer my question," he gritted, keeping up the furious charade. "What are you doing here?"

She laughed nervously. "It seems your friends at MI6 think I ought to help you with your little project. They told me to work with you or go to jail." She hesitated fractionally and then continued in a more sober tone of voice. "I'm sorry they forced me to bother you."

Surprised by what sounded like a genuine apology, he eased up leaning on her. She immediately turned to face him within the cage of his arms. She breathed, "I forgot just how big you are."

Pleasure erupted in his gut before he managed to check the reaction. He scowled. The woman definitely knew how to work the sex angle. He muttered, "I thought we already established that you can't do the job."

"You decided that. MI6 thinks I'm up to the challenge. Are you?"

Their gazes met and held. Her big, green, long-lashed eyes were even more seductive than they had been in the restaurant. With each breath she drew, her chest rubbed the front of his shirt. She seemed fully aware of it and prepared to maintain the blatantly sexual contact. An urge to carry her inside and untie that naughty little dress slammed into him. Damn, she was dangerous.

"I can handle anything you can dish out and then some, sweetheart," he murmured.

Her hands came up to rest on his forearms, her fingers sliding higher to measure his biceps, and then gliding across his chest and down his belly to his belt. He sucked in an involuntary breath as her hands skimmed the leather barrier.

"Are you sure about that?" she murmured back, eyes sparkling, her voice thick with sexual innuendo.

He leaned in on her, crowding her, forcing her to acknowledge his superior size and power. Her hands slid around his waist to the small of his back, her palms—whether consciously or unconsciously he didn't know—urging him closer still. He could just imagine her gripping him, pulling him to her, rising up to meet his thrusts as he pumped into her.

His gaze refocused on her face and, dammit, she was smiling archly. He speared a hand into her hair and grabbed a thick handful. He forced her head back, exposing her graceful throat. "Don't play with me, little girl. You may get more than you bargained for."

His intent had been to intimidate her, threaten her a little. But damned if her eyes didn't go dark and hot, her whole body limp with lust against his. Desire rolled off of her like heat waves off a beach in the noonday sun. Liked it a little rough, did she? The knowledge exploded through his brain, along with any number of forbidden possibilities.

"Gahh," he grunted as he shoved away from her. "Using sex won't work for this mission. Like I said. You're going to get yourself—and maybe me—killed. I don't need a sex kitten. I need a real woman."

He turned his back on her and strode to the far end of the porch to stare out into the night. He did his damnedest to ignore the blood pounding through his body and roaring in his ears, but he failed. The woman was sin incarnate. But his declaration was true. He didn't need a high-class hooker wannabe. He needed a terrorist wannabe.

"Try me," she murmured from right behind him. "Maybe I *am* a real woman."

How in the hell had she managed to sneak up on him like that? How was he supposed to train her if she distracted him this much?

He whirled to glare at her. "You have no idea what you're getting yourself into."

"Then explain it to me."

Even when she wasn't trying to be sexy, she was. Her mouth formed words and he stared at her lush lips, thinking of all the indecent things he could do with that mouth.

"Grab your bags and come inside," he growled. "The supply plane won't be here until day after tomorrow. Until then, you're stuck on the island."

He caught her little smile of triumph as she turned to fetch her luggage. His plan had worked to perfection. She thought she'd talked him into letting her stay—at least for long enough to convince him she could do his mission, which she now desperately wanted to do. He ought to feel like he'd delivered the knock-out punch. But instead, he felt like the one who'd just taken a barrage of body blows.

How in the hell was he supposed to keep his hands off her for weeks or even months to come? If she unleashed a full broadside of sex appeal at him, he wasn't at all sure he would come out the winner—or if he even wanted to come out the winner.

Eve mentally girded herself as she sat down to eat the supper Brady had prepared for them. She had two days to convince him she had what it took to do his mission. It would make her ultimate refusal to help him all that much sweeter revenge. She would be truly nuts to pursue working with this man for real. He'd already told her if she screwed up she might die. And he didn't strike her as the kind of person to exaggerate.

As Brady plated up the largest prawns she'd ever seen on a bed of pasta and some sort of delicate cream sauce, she studied him closely. He wasn't intimidating until a person noticed how silently and efficiently he moved. Like a killer. A chill rippled down her spine.

"So, Brady. Can you tell me about your secret mission now that we're completely alone?"

"I'm going to put you through a little training to see if you're even capable of pulling it off. If it looks like you could get the job done, then I'll tell you more about it."

She leaned back, studying him thoughtfully. "Don't trust me, huh? Worried I'll tell on you to my secret terrorist friends?"

"Something like that," he allowed.

"Fair enough. But for the record, I really did have no idea what dear brother Viktor was up to, and I had no part in his little projects."

"For the record, I believe you."

She stared at him in open surprise. "Thank you."

"You're welcome."

Her plate was almost clean when he surprised her by saying without preamble, "I can't tell you much, but I can tell you this: the mission is dangerous. I would act as your handler, which I hasten to add before you can make any snide comment, merely means that you would be working for me and I would provide whatever support you'd need. If you were to succeed, you would clear your family name once and for all. If you were to fail, you would almost certainly die."

Clear the family name? The idea broke across her consciousness like an avalanche, sweeping away everything in its path. Was it possible? Was he for real? Then the rest of it sunk in. She would work for him? That could be very interesting indeed. But then there was that whole dying thing to consider—

"I hear your mental wheels turning," he said quickly. "Don't get worked up over the prospect of restoring the family name. I'm not kidding. You can't pull off the mission."

But if she could…a fresh start in life…doing his mission might just be worth it… "Who do you work for, Mr. Hathaway?"

"Why do you ask?"

"Because I'd like to tell them you're the worst recruiter I've ever had the misfortune to encounter. And believe me, I've met a whole lot of your type."

He studied her for long enough that she had to restrain an urge to squirm in her seat. Then he merely leaned forward with a sinfully wicked smile and said, "You want to give it a go then?"

Hell, yes, she wanted to give it a go! She leaned back, feigning casual disdain, and drawled, "I suppose I've got nothing better to do."

Brady let out a careful breath. Why did he feel like he'd just grabbed a tiger by the tail? The woman seated across from him was even more fantastically beautiful in person than she was on film. Her mind worked at lightning speed, and she was as prickly and cynical as they came.

But he could no more let go of the tiger's tail than he could walk away from the sexual challenge glinting in her green gaze. She was going to be hell on wheels to manage. He had no illusions whatsoever about why she'd agreed to do the mission: she was determined to win the charged sexual battle snapping and sparking between them.

However, he also had faith that the emotional pain pouring off of her in tangible waves was going to be extremely difficult and delicate to manage. He wondered if she had any idea how much pain she radiated.

He was dead serious when he said she was completely unsuited to the mission at hand. How he was going to mold her into any kind of reasonably functional operative, he had no idea. Not to mention the thought of being alone with her made his gut tighten involuntarily.

And now she was officially a mission. Work. Off-limits. He was supposed to be the confirmed woman hater, the man of ice. It was why Jennifer had asked him to handle this particular job. Time to put some of that mental chill to work.

She startled him out of his musings by asking, "So what is this training of yours going to entail?"

"Ever shoot a gun?" he asked.

"No."

"Wire a bomb?"

"No."

"Kill someone?"

"No!"

"Well, then," he said lightly. "We've got our work cut out for us." He blandly turned his attention back to his meal.

Her fork clattered down onto her plate. "You want me to kill someone?" she gasped. "I'd never kill anyone. Not for you. Not for anyone!"

He stared into her horrified eyes and answered quietly, "I will never force you to kill anyone. But there are scenarios where everyone would find themselves willing to take a life. Don't fool yourself that you'd never do it. In the right circumstances you wouldn't hesitate."

"Never," she declared strongly.

His gaze narrowed. "You're telling me that if you had a loaded gun in your hand you'd let a criminal kill your husband? Rape your daughter? Torture your baby?"

"That's not a fair example. Nothing like that will ever happen to me."

"Never say never, Miss Dupont."

"Call me Eve," she snapped.

Good. He had her rattled. She needed to realize a little of what she was getting into. He didn't need her accusing him later of misleading her. He replied grimly, "Call me Brady. We're going to be working very closely for the next few months. We might as well dispense with the formalities."

"Done…Brady." Triumph glinted in her eyes.

Ha. She thought she'd just manipulated him into agreeing to work with her. He smiled sardonically. Whatever got the job done. And in the meantime, was that a hint of a truce showing on her oh so expressive face?

"Why didn't you ask if I'd kill you if I had a gun?" she asked sweetly.

So much for a truce. He snorted. "I already know the answer to that one," he answered grimly.

Eve helped carry the dishes into the kitchen and clean up. After they were done, she couldn't resist the night breezes drawing her to the porch. She stepped out into the sultry darkness. She felt Brady join her, although she didn't hear him.

"You should get a good night's sleep," he murmured.

"We'll get an early start in the morning and work hard all day."

"Are you telling me the truth?" she asked. "Is there really a mission?"

"Yes. There really is."

"Tell me something, Mr. Honesty with a capital H. Do you find me attractive?"

"What makes you think I always tell the truth?"

Avoiding her question, was he? Interesting. Aloud she replied, "Oh, come on. You've got a neon sign over your head that says All-American Boy. Of course you always tell the truth. You keep your promises and help little old ladies cross the street, too."

"I leave little old ladies to the Boy Scouts," he muttered.

"You dodged my question. Do you find me attractive?"

He stared at her through narrowed eyes. "You're extremely attractive, but you don't need me to tell you that."

"That's not what I asked." She turned to face him, and he was wreathed in dark shadows that hid his face. "Do *you* find me attractive?"

"Such things have no bearing on the mission," he answered tightly.

"So you do. Why won't you admit it?"

"We're going to be working together very closely. Exploring such issues would make things…awkward…between us."

"Things are pretty awkward already," she retorted. "I think we should get whatever's between us out in the open and deal with it like adults rather than letting all this sexual tension just hang in the air as if it's not there."

He turned his head slightly, enough for her to see his jaw muscles rippling. Score a bull's-eye for her.

"I don't think that's a good idea—" he started.

She stepped close to him. "It may not be a good idea, but you and I both know it's inevitable."

"Nothing's inevitable," he retorted a little more sharply than was necessary.

"Shut up and kiss me," she breathed.

His arms swept around her and he wrapped her in an embrace that made her feel by turns safe and entirely consumed. And then his mouth closed on hers, and any thought of missions or verbal sparring evaporated. He didn't kiss her as much as he inhaled her. This was no tentative request for permission to worship her. It was mastery, at once tender and powerful.

Whoa. Wait a minute. The idea was for *her* to sweep *him* off his feet. To assert her control in this relationship, not the other way around! But darned if she didn't urge him closer, her lips clinging hungrily to his, her body pulsing with need.

She didn't get all hot and bothered by kisses—she was the one who made other people feel that way. But darned if she wasn't panting for breath, drowning in his strength and already trying to figure out how to get more of him. Her legs actually felt weak as an unfamiliar languor stole through her.

She wanted him to strip off her dress and put his hands on her skin. To carry her down and cover her with his big body. To take her places she'd never thought about going with a man before. Usually boredom was her primary emotion when guys started crawling all over her. But Brady made her feel hungry. Restless. Crud...*horny.*

He turned her loose so abruptly she staggered before righting herself on wobbly legs. His expression was inscrutable, his posture casual. "All right, then," he said briskly. "Now that we've got that out of the way, we can get to work first thing in the morning."

She stared in disbelief. Surely that kiss had affected him the same way it had affected her! Then why was he studying her like an insect again, one eyebrow cocked in mild disdain. Seriously? That kiss hadn't rocked his world?

Hurt flashed for an instant before white hot rage exploded inside her. "You son of a bitch!"

"You're the one who insisted on kissing," he replied blandly.

And then he actually turned and walked away from her! Just like that. As if kissing her hadn't been any more interesting than reading obituaries in the newspaper. If she wasn't mistaken, he was smirking.

Her hands balled into fists that ached to bury themselves in his smug expression. He'd played her like a freaking violin! He thought he could kiss her and get her all worked up and then turn and walk away all superior and unaffected, did he? Well she had news for him. He wouldn't know which way was up when she was done with him. She wouldn't have him begging at her feet; she'd have him groveling at her feet before she was done with him. He wanted a war of the sexes? Then war it would be. Her mouth curved up into an anticipatory smile. Brady Hathaway wasn't going to know what had hit him.

Chapter 3

"This is a pistol," Brady lectured. "This is a bullet. Individually, neither is dangerous. But put one inside the other, and together, they form a lethal combination."

He caught Eve's gaze snapping to his, searching for a double meaning. Satisfaction reverberated in his gut. She wanted to run around tempting and teasing him? Two could play that game. He continued his lesson as he disassembled the weapon and showed her its interior workings.

"So far, so good," Eve murmured.

"Okay. Your turn." He passed her the weapon and she made a sound of surprise at its weight that sent a shiver down his spine. Yet again, she wasn't trying to be sexy, but oh, how she was. Or maybe that was just him overreacting.

"So how do I shoot this thing?" she asked.

"First you spread your legs."

Her gaze shot to his in minor shock.

"For stability in your stance, of course," he explained.

"Arms straight out in front of you at shoulder height." He added slyly, "Grip the butt tightly. Hold on no matter what it does in your hands. It'll buck hard, but don't let go. Got it?"

Her sage-green eyes went so hot and bothered he barely managed not to laugh. He continued gravely, "Don't do anything jerky with your hands. It throws off the weapon's aim, and that can get messy."

She all but choked at that graphic imagery while he all but choked on his amusement. "Ready to give it a go?" he purred. "It won't hurt, I promise."

"Um, sure."

Ha. She sounded rattled. Off balance. He spoke low, his voice charged. "Squeeze smooth and slow. Once you start your stroke, go all the way. Don't pull back or stop part way. Go until you feel the trigger guard."

She looked strangely overheated as she swallowed hard, aimed and fired.

The weapon in her hand made a mighty explosion of light and sound. But instead of letting it kick up into the air, Eve fought the recoil and tried to hold the gun level. In retaliation, the weapon sent its energy backward instead of up. It knocked her, in no uncertain terms, on her bum.

Brady burst out laughing.

"Ow!" Eve glared up at him. "You could've warned me it was going to do that."

"Welcome to Sir Isaac Newton's first law of motion: for every action, there's an equal and opposite reaction." Sort of like the two of them. She pushed, he pushed back. She flirted, he flirted back. Yep. Just nature taking its inevitable course.

He reached a hand down to her. Their palms met. Intense anticipation passed through him, not unlike when he kissed her last night. He tugged her to her feet, grinning down at her for an instant before turning her loose.

She demanded indignantly, "How is anyone supposed to control a beast like that and actually hit anything with it?"

He whipped his own pistol out of its holster and into a firing position and proceeded to plant five rounds in the target twenty-five yards away in a tight cluster the size of a quarter. "Like that," he replied blandly.

"Show off."

Maybe a little. He shrugged. "It's all a matter of practice and focus. Although it helps that I'm a man and stronger than you."

She harrumphed under her breath and tipped her chin at the target with its tattered hole in the middle of the bull's-eye. "How did you do that?"

Aah. Her competitive impulses were kicking in. These he could work with. "You're at a disadvantage because of your lack of upper body strength compared to mine." As he'd expected, her brows came together at that comment. She focused intently as he explained how to sight and aim. Clearly, she intended to show him a girl could be just as good at this as a boy. She really was too easy to manipulate.

She fired at the target paper and peppered shots all over the target. She swore under her breath in French and reloaded her weapon. Again, her shots went wild.

"What am I doing wrong?" she demanded.

He moved around behind her. "Take your shooting stance."

He stepped close behind her, wrapping his arms around her from behind, his hands closing over her fists as she held the weapon. If he wasn't mistaken, a fine trembling passed through her.

Grinning, he murmured, "Spread your legs a little more. Brace your hips." He nudged her pelvis with his. "Feel how you have to stiffen up against me to keep your balance?"

She made a choked sound he'd take as a yes.

"Now, feel how I'm pushing with my weapon hand and

pulling with my off hand?" She nodded, and a fresh floral scent rose off her hair. He was tempted to bury his face in it. "It's the push-pull that makes the whole thing work."

Yep. Women and guns. They were just alike. Complex, beautiful and dangerous.

"Now you try it," he directed.

She breathed out, her body going still and relaxed against his, her hands tensed within his. Her index finger flexed. *Bang!* The impact flung her back against him.

"Um, sorry," she mumbled.

"Are you closing your eyes just before you pull the trigger?" he asked.

"No."

"Are you sure? Try again, but concentrate on keeping your eyes open."

This time the weapon remained steady in her hands and she hit the black ring between the nine and ten circles. "It worked!" she cried.

"Funny how watching when you do something makes it better."

She commented absently as she lined up another shot, "I've always found that to be true with sex, too."

His hands tightened convulsively around hers and her shot went wide. "Hey! That was your fault. You jerked my hands."

"You're the one who brought up sex. Your fault the shot went wild."

She glanced sidelong at him over her shoulder. "You haven't even begun to see wild...yet."

And just like that, the scales were even, sexual tension vibrating through both of them, as stifling as the tropical humidity.

He stepped back, his arms falling away from her. "Try it by yourself."

"But I don't like doing it alone," she pouted. "It's more fun with a partner."

His gaze narrowed. Laughing, she turned to face the target. She fired until she was wincing and shaking her hand and he made her stop.

Next, she needed to learn how to handle explosives. He explained the basic mechanism of wiring and detonation, and Eve grasped the concept lightning fast. She had a natural gift for bomb-making. In less than an hour, she knew how to make several basic improvised explosive devices.

As she finished wiring a timer device to a block of training C-4—mostly inert putty with only a tiny amount of the actual explosive embedded within it—she asked, "When do we get to blow up something?"

"Who'd have guessed you're such a pyromaniac?"

"That's me. I'm all about fireworks."

Their laughing gazes met, and the humor drained quickly from the moment, replaced by simmering heat. *Ice, dammit.* He tore his gaze away from hers and said, "These aren't real explosives, but they'll give you an idea what the concussion of high explosives are like. Unwind that reel of det cord and lay a line of it over there to that fallen tree. We'll take cover behind it."

She followed his directions, and in a few moments they crouched behind the big log.

"Would you like to do the honors?" he asked. She smiled eagerly and he passed her the remote control. "Whenever you're ready, push the red button."

Her eyes lit up with pleasure and something unfamiliar tugged at his heart. He liked making her happy. Before he could consider the implications of that, a tremendous blast of sound and heat slammed into them.

She lurched violently, banging into his side. "My God," she breathed. "Let's do it again."

His gut clenched so hard it hurt. He could thing of several things he'd like to do with her repeatedly. She needed to stop saying things like that or else he was going to be tempted to act on the invitation in her voice.

He spoke evenly, but it cost him a lot to control his tone. "Tomorrow I'll show you how to daisy chain multiple detonations, and we'll blow up some more stuff."

"Promise?"

"Promise," he answered firmly. Who'd have guessed the high-fashion blonde would be such a bomb freak? She might just pull off this mission, after all. Assuming he could keep his hands off of her long enough to train her. If the original Eve had been half this attractive, no wonder Adam had fallen for her charms.

After lunch, Eve changed into an airy white gauze dress for the afternoon's academic session. She was glad to stay in the air conditioning and avoid the intense heat outside. Although she couldn't imagine what Brady had to teach her about death and destruction from a textbook.

He was seated on the sofa when she came into the living room, wearing crisply pressed khakis and a white polo shirt.

"Do you ever look messy?" she asked curiously.

"It's not uncommon for me to be covered in mud, leaves and camouflage paint during a mission."

"Am I going to have to do that?" she asked.

"I doubt it. You're more likely to have to blend in on an expensive beach in the Cayman Islands."

"Aah, well. I'm pretty good at beaches."

His eyes went hot and turbulent. "I know. I've seen a picture of you in a skimpy bikini."

Amusement flashed through her. And maybe that explained a bit of his tension around her. Although the two of them were generating plenty of sparks without any skimpy bikinis in sight. "So what's on the agenda this afternoon, Professor Death?"

He gestured for her to sit. She ignored the chair across from him and instead chose the far end of the sofa he sat on. His jaw tightened and she chalked up another score for her in the battle of the sexes. He'd gotten in a few excellent shots this morning, and she had some getting even to do. Recollection of his powerful arms around her as he taught her how to shoot sent a strange little shiver through her.

It really was odd how she reacted to him. She wasn't a big fan of men in general, and particularly not of sex with them. People assumed that because she was beautiful and sultry-looking that she lived and died for sex, but that couldn't be further from the truth. But around Brady…she actually was experiencing an unfamiliar flare of interest.

She blinked, focusing on the man a few feet away. He was leaning back, watching her intently, his eyes a stormy shade of gray this afternoon. "What?" she asked.

"Care to share what was on your mind just then?"

"Why do you ask?" She was curious to know what he thought he'd seen.

"That was an interesting sequence of facial expressions. I don't know how to interpret them," he replied.

"Just as well you not know."

That sent one dark eyebrow slashing up. "Here's the thing, Eve. You and I are going to be working very closely together, potentially in some very high stress situations. We need to be able to trust each other, possibly with our lives. If you want to do this, you're going to have to open up to me. I'll certainly keep any personal information you reveal to myself. But secrets aren't going to cut it between us."

No secrets, huh? Apprehension shouted like an alarm clock in her gut. "Then we have a small problem," she retorted. "My life is all about secrets. I don't let anybody inside my guard."

"So I've noticed." He leaned forward. "You have a decision to make, then. Do you want this bad enough to let me in?"

"I don't even know that *this* is," she snapped.

He shrugged. "It's redemption. A clean slate for you. Your life given back to you."

She closed her eyes. How was it he knew exactly what bait to dangle to most tempt her? "But I didn't do anything wrong," she whispered.

"Your name is Dupont. How many people believe you when you say that?"

She smacked her hand down on the coffee table. "But I didn't do anything, dammit!"

"I know that. You know that. I'm offering you a chance to prove it to everyone else."

They both knew she wouldn't say no to the offer. Couldn't say no. Damn Viktor anyway, she thought tiredly. He and this man before her had both trapped her as neatly as any rabbit in a snare. She looked up at Brady bleakly. "I hate being forced into anything."

He leaned back, his expression closed. "I'm not forcing you. I'm offering you an opportunity. Your choice."

"You know as well as I do that I have no choice at all. MI6 twisting my arm or not, I had to come here. I have to do this."

He nodded, smiling slowly. "That wasn't so hard, now, was it?"

"What wasn't?"

"Being honest with me. The sky didn't fall, and I don't think any worse of you."

Why did she get the feeling he'd just manipulated her into saying exactly what he wanted her to say?

He reached down beside the sofa and laid a very large, very scary looking weapon on the coffee table. "This is a sniper gun. A small one, but probably about as big as you can handle with your limited upper body strength."

He commenced lecturing her on how it worked and how to disassemble and reassemble it. Before long, the thing lay in pieces all over the coffee table while he quizzed her about what each part did and where it went.

No secrets between them? Her mind kept circling back to that one. That could be tough. She'd never known anyone with whom she could be completely honest. Maybe if Victor had lived past her teens they might have become confidants. But she'd just been coming into herself when he'd been killed. By men like Brady Hathaway.

Her mother had lost herself in gin after Viktor died. No maternal shoulder to share her secrets with there. The police, the media, their friends and neighbors—everyone had been sure she'd known what Viktor was up to. Her mother might have had some clue, but not her. Never her. It turned out he'd had as many secrets as she had.

"Earth to Eve, come in."

Startled, she glanced up. "Did I mess something up?"

"Not at all. Which is impressive, given how distracted you were. Whenever you're around a lethal weapon, safety demands that you keep your total attention on it."

She sighed. "Sorry."

"How about we get out of here? Go for a swim?"

"That sounds great." Her body was nearly as restless as her mind this afternoon.

She changed into one of her skimpy bikinis, smirking. He might get inside her head, but she knew exactly how to get inside his, too. Mr. Hathaway had an Achilles' heel of his own—he was a red-blooded male and couldn't quite stop himself from reacting to her as one.

He was waiting for her in the golf cart when she stepped outside. His jaw clenched with an entirely satisfying ripple when he saw her. He drove to the beach in silence, which she would interpret as a win for her. Pleased with how the battle

of the sexes was unfolding, she sat back to enjoy the view…
of both the island and the man beside her.

Brady gripped the steering wheel so hard he must be
leaving dents in it. The woman radiated smugness, and
with good reason. How could any man see her in a few
scraps of cloth and string and not think about torrid sex? He
sent distinctly homicidal thoughts in Jennifer Blackfoot's
direction.

He parked at the edge of the small, white sand beach on
the north end of the island. Eve squealed in delight and took
off running for the water. She splashed out into the surf and
when she was thigh-deep knifed into the water in a running
dive. She swam out to sea with long, efficient strokes. Yep.
A natural in the water.

He followed more slowly. He frankly could use a little
distance from her to catch his breath. She'd swum off to his
left, paralleling the beach, and he followed after her. She
eventually turned around to head back and he did the same.
They swam side-by-side for the nearly half-mile back to the
beach. She waded ashore, panting, and flopped into the sand
under a palm tree.

He sat down beside her, resting an elbow on a bent knee
and staring out to sea.

"What's on your mind?" she asked, surprising him. He
glanced down at her and she added, "Trust is a two-way
street, right? If you want me to tell you my secrets, surely I
have a right to expect the same from you."

He wasn't crazy about baring his soul to this mercurial
woman he barely knew. Hell, he wouldn't bare his soul to
some woman he knew inside and out. Females were chaotic
creatures who made for messy entanglements. He much
preferred the life he'd built for himself without women in
it—orderly, predictable and quiet.

She nodded knowingly. "That's what I thought. What's good for the goose isn't all right for the gander."

"I'm your handler, not your boyfriend."

She jerked back looking stung. "Is that what this is about? Sleeping with me?"

It was his turn to jerk. "Not at all. I have no intention of sleeping with you."

"You're sure about that?"

His gaze snapped to hers. Contemplating a thing and acting upon it were two entirely separate matters. What was that in her voice, anyway? It certainly wasn't a note of seduction. Cynicism, maybe? "Is it so hard for you to believe a man might be able to keep his hands off you?"

She shrugged. "You haven't kept your hands off me."

"You kissed me," he flared up. "I only kissed you back."

"And if I kiss you again? Would you kiss me back and then call the whole thing my fault?"

"Why are you so determined to push sex between us?" he challenged.

"Because it's always there between me and men. Especially good-looking, virile men who are used to having whatever woman they want."

She thought he was good-looking and virile, huh? "I don't 'have' whatever woman I want. I have a demanding career that takes up most of my time. And even if I had time, I'm not interested in most women."

Particularly sexy women who threw themselves at men. He'd endured his mother's addiction to sex as a kid and had nothing but contempt for women like her. She'd gotten every little scrap of self-esteem she managed to pull together from the men who used her and tossed her away like trash. Technically, she hadn't been a hooker. But she'd supplemented her income as a receptionist heavily by pawning the gifts her many boyfriends gave to her. It had been a humiliating way to grow up, knowing his mother was sleeping her way to rent and food on the table.

Eve was speaking again. "…but you are interested in me. I was there when you kissed me back, remember?"

She wasn't going to let him forget that, was she? He replied evenly, "You were also there when I ended the kiss and walked away."

That sent a shadow of hurt through her light green gaze, which in turn knotted his gut unpleasantly. He reminded himself that, at the end of the day, she was the one doing him the favor by infiltrating Annika's cell, not the other way around.

He sighed and changed the subject. "The mission is going to put you in the path of some dangerous and violent people. I'm worried about you."

"How so?"

Thank God she was going along with the change of subject. He really didn't want to have to hurt her any more. That look in her eye said she'd suffered more of it in her life than most people were aware of.

"I'd suggest you be careful about provoking the men you'll be hanging around. They could be…brutes."

"You mean they might try to rape me?" She shrugged as if unimpressed by the prospect.

Really worried now, he glared down at her. He'd listened to his mother cry in her bedroom more than once after one of her male guests played a little too rough. "I'm serious, Eve."

"Sex has always been about power and always will be. If some guy decides he needs to have his way with me to show how powerful he is, whatever."

Brady's jaw literally dropped. "Excuse me?"

She stared up at him equal parts surprised and defiant. "What?" she demanded.

"You don't care if someone assaults you?" he asked incredulously.

"Isn't that basically what sex is anyway?"

"Good Lord. What kind of sex have you had to think that?" She opened her mouth as if to answer and he threw up his hands. "Never mind. I don't want to know."

She shrugged.

He jumped up and paced along the beach, kicking idly at the wavelets as they rolled in. No wonder she was such a cynic. Did she really believe sex was at best a power play and at worst an attack women were supposed to endure?

His cell phone vibrated. "Hathaway," he said irritably.

"Hey, it's Jennifer. I see you two are taking a break from training. How's it going with your girl?"

Eve was emphatically *not* his girl. He barely stopped himself from snapping that to his colleague. Instead, he blurted, "Do all women think sex is basically an act of assault?"

"Do I want to know why you're bringing this up?" Jennifer sounded startled.

"Trying to figure out Eve. She's not exactly what I expected."

"Has she been raped? Is she too unstable for this op? Do we need to scrub her and wait for a Medusa to cut loose?"

"I don't think we have that long before Annika strikes again," Brady replied. "I'm not ready to give up on Eve. She's just more of a man-hater than I pegged her for."

"With looks like that?" Jennifer half-laughed. "No surprise. Men can act like colossal jerks around pretty women. She's probably been pawed by the worst of them."

"So I'm gathering," he replied dryly.

"Hang in there. You men aren't all bad eggs. Take you, for example. You don't make passes at women no matter now hot they are."

"Do you have anything work related you want to tell me," he ground out, "or is this call purely meant to insult and harass me?"

"We're getting pressure from the families of the Americans who were killed in the Dred-Naught bombing—and their various elected representatives—to arrest someone. I've been trying to explain that there's not enough evidence to charge anyone with any crime and that I'm trying to collect it. But congressmen with dead constituents want someone to blame right away, proof or no proof."

"Hold your ground," he advised. "Making an arrest right now would be useless. They'll just have to be patient. You might want to tell the journalists on the story to cool their jets, too."

"Easier said than done," Jennifer grumbled.

He laughed. "That's why they pay you the big bucks."

She snorted. "What big bucks? I'm a government employee."

"I'll call you if anything changes down here, Jenn."

"Good luck…and hurry."

He disconnected the call. Good luck, indeed. He'd need more than that to deal with Eve Dupont. He'd need a damned miracle to come out of this op unscathed.

Chapter 4

Eve watched Brady pocket his phone and head back in her direction, scowling. Why was he so bothered by her cavalier attitude toward men? Did he actually give a damn about her? Care about her feelings? Surely not. It wasn't how men were wired. Once they stopped thinking with their brains and started thinking with their...well, *not* thinking at all...they all turned into colossal jerks. Brady wouldn't be any different.

He sat down beside her and stared out to sea, tension radiating from him. "What's got you so wired?" she asked. "That phone call?"

His gaze didn't leave the ocean. "My colleague was urging me to hurry."

"Hurry what?"

"Your preparation for this mission. Thing is, I'm still not sure I want to send you out."

"What's the hang-up? Is it me...or is it you?"

That finally got him to look at her. But his gaze was distant. Inscrutable. "That is the question, isn't it?"

"All right. We've established the question. What's the answer, then?"

Frowning, he picked up a bit of a sea shell idly and tossed it toward the ocean. "I'm worried about you going out in the field by yourself. You're totally unprepared for what you're going to face. Of course, that's exactly why you'll succeed. I can't even give you the most basic training, or our target will spot you and kill you."

She turned over that information in her mind. So, she was being sent on a mission precisely because of her ignorance. Great. As for her being unable to deal with whatever happened, she commented, "I didn't grow up in some utopian paradise, you know. I survived the mean streets of a violence-prone region. There were bombings and clashes with police, Basque separatists who'd kill you if you didn't support them, and French loyalists who'd kill you if you did. And as you've been at pains to point out, it wasn't like I had caring parents or even a protective brother to look out for me. I mostly figured it out on my own."

He shook his head in denial.

She pressed further. "Has it occurred to you that I'm not some fragile, helpless thing? It just so happens I've been taking care of myself for a good long time. And I'm still standing."

"I can guarantee you've never been in the kind of danger I'm about to put you in. This mission may very well be too much for you."

"We won't know until we try, will we?"

"The price of failure could be your death, and possibly mine. And that changes everything—for you at least. You're a civilian."

"Civilians aren't allowed to risk their lives for something

they believe in? Only you military types are allowed to do that? Is that how your world works?"

"Yes. It is. It's my job to protect people like you."

She sat up beside him. "People like me? Exactly how stupid do you think I am?"

"I don't think you're the slightest bit stupid. But you've got no idea—"

She cut him off. "Then give me a little credit for being able to figure it out as I go."

"You're determined to do this come hell or high water, aren't you?" he demanded.

"You offered me a shot at getting my life back. Wild horses won't stop me from taking that shot. It's too late for you to back out of this now. We're both committed. Even your boss is telling you to hurry."

"She's not my boss. We're coworkers."

"She? You work with a woman?" Eve hadn't seen that one coming. Why then, was he so hinky about putting her out in the field? "C'mon, Brady. Quit…how do you say it…cat footing around."

"Pussyfooting," he answered dryly. "Fine. You're determined to do this mission no matter what? So be it."

"Thank God," she breathed. "So. Tell me the details."

He snorted. "Your mission is to infiltrate a terrorist cell led by your dead brother's ex-lover, Annika Cantori. I believe you know her?"

Annika. The name flowed through Eve like bitter poison, conjuring a face from her distant past. A hard, frightening young woman who'd lured Viktor into the world of violence and extremism that ultimately killed him.

"She recruited my brother," Eve said in a strangled voice she hardly recognized as her own. Memories of the skinny, short-haired, punked-out, preternaturally intense girl who had taken her brother from her rolled through Eve's mind.

"And now you're going to let her recruit you," Brady continued. "In fact, you're going to do everything in your power to get her to recruit you. You want to take up the work with her where your brother left off."

With her brother's lover. The woman her mother had always blamed for Viktor's death. Eve agreed with her mother: Annika was also her brother's killer. And she was supposed to work with the woman? Surely not. Aloud, she asked, "Am I supposed to kill her?"

"No. You're just supposed to find out if she's responsible for the nightclub bombing in Jamaica last week and discover what she's planning next. I'll arrest her once you've gotten the evidence I need."

"You don't arrest a woman like Annika. She'll never be taken alive." An image of her brother, laughing and teasing her, flashed through Eve's brain. He'd made an intolerable life tolerable for her. He'd looked out for her. Taken care of her. Until Annika. He'd become a stranger—moody and distant and dark. And then he'd died on a suicide mission engineered by Annika. And she was supposed to work with the woman? No way. Kill her, yes. Cooperate with her? Not a chance.

"How well, exactly, do you know her?" Brady asked, sounding suspicious all of a sudden.

She thought fast. Brady knew where Annika was. Had resources that could help her get close to the woman. If she wanted to kill Annika, she'd have to play along for now.

Eve answered lightly, "I know her very well, of course. She's from my hometown, which wasn't much more than a village. Everyone knew everyone. How do you think she and Viktor met?" Eve shrugged, trying to look casual. "Her little brother, Drago, was in my grade in school. Awful boy. Sick in the head. Used to invent horrible ways to kill mice to gross out us girls."

Brady jolted. "We have no record of her having a brother. Do you know where he is now?"

"The way I heard it, he was shot and killed on the cruise ship at the same time you people killed my brother." She halted, checking her bitterness. Not the way to get Brady to use her on his mission. She added hastily, "Trust me. Drago Cantori was no loss to the world. He was a psychopath."

"What about Annika?" Brady asked eagerly. "What was she like as a child? Our profilers are going to have a field day with this. They rarely get detailed background information on a subject's childhood."

Eve opened her mouth to speak, but Brady waved her to silence. "Wait a second before you answer." He pulled out his cell phone and spoke into it quickly. "Jennifer, you're never going to believe this. Eve knew Annika and her brother as kids. I'll put her on speakerphone."

There was a short delay while some sort of recording device was activated on the other end, and then a woman with a rich contralto voice announced, "Whenever Eve's ready."

Reluctantly, Eve thought back to a time she rarely allowed herself to visit in her mind. "Alberto Cantori—Annika's father—was a leader in the Basque separatist movement. A violent man. He gradually grew more unhinged as we grew up. Used to beat up his wife and kids. Annika and Drago would show up at school with black eyes and split lips often. The story was always that they were studying martial arts."

Eve remembered feeling sorry for Annika until the day she'd said something to the older girl about it and gotten spit on for her trouble. She continued, "Annika and Drago were throwing Molotov cocktails at army troops by the time they were eight or so."

"Did they get arrested?" Brady asked.

"They were always in trouble with the police. But they were so young. No one wanted to throw them in jail. They usually got hauled home to their mother. She was a decent enough woman, if not very bright. Ran a laundry."

A male voice from the phone said, "Tell us more about the father."

Eve glanced at Brady, who nodded encouragingly. "I was scared of him. He had a crazy look in his eye. Like he was always half-considering how to kill you. I never knew if he was that committed to a Basque homeland or if he just used it as an excuse for violence. Rumor had it he got nearly beaten to death by the police as a young man and was never quite right in the head after that."

"What did Annika think of her father?" Brady prompted when she stopped speaking.

Eve frowned. Viktor would have known the answer to that one, but she wasn't so sure. "My impression is that she both loved and hated him. Is that too vague?"

"Not at all." Brady smiled at her. "Go on. What else can you remember?"

"The kids at school nearly worshipped Annika. You have to understand. None of us liked the police or the military. We all sympathized with the freedom fighters. Not to mention, she had tattoos and wore black leather pants and had facial piercings. She was a rebel who infuriated our teachers. Of course we all thought she was cool."

The man again. "Would you say the locals protected Annika and her family?"

Eve answered without hesitation, "Absolutely. No matter what they saw her or her family do. No one in town would talk to the French police. They were the enemy."

"That's our entrée," Brady announced. "Eve is someone Annika can trust because she already has a history of keeping her mouth shut about the Cantori family to the police." He threw her a sidelong look. "And Eve's never given the authorities anything to work with regarding Viktor's death."

"That's because I don't know anything!" she protested.

The man on the phone piped up. "But Annika doesn't know that. Eve can intimate that her brother spoke freely to her, and she has protected his secrets all these years. Annika will respond well to that."

Sick dread roiled in her gut at the idea of lying to Annika. The girl got that same homicidal look in her eyes that her father used to. And she'd beaten the hell out of the only girl in school who'd dared cross her. That had been one of the few times Annika had spent some time in the local jail. After Viktor died, who knew how crazy she'd gotten? He'd always been a stabilizing influence on her—which was a scary thought, given that he'd ultimately died in a terrorist attack himself.

The psychologist/profiler, or whatever he was, continued, "If Eve appears to have transferred hero worship of her dead brother to his ex-lover, that will seem logical to Annika. Even a chance sighting of Annika, alive and well when everyone thinks she's dead, would plausibly trigger the transference of idolization."

Eve frowned. "If you want me to work with Annika, pretty much all I'll have to do is invoke my brother. Viktor saved Annika's life. I'll just call in that debt."

"How did Viktor save her?" Brady asked, startled.

"She tangled with the French army one time too many. They came looking for her. She made it out of her house and into the street where they tried to gun her down. Viktor dived in front of her and took three bullets to the gut."

She'd never forget the horror of that day, the sound of the shots, the screams of the bystanders, the blood. So much blood. And Annika, just standing there, staring down at her brother like he was roadkill. It had been Annika's mother who leaped forward, tearing off a strip of her skirt and pressing it to Viktor's wounds to staunch the bleeding until an ambulance arrived. Eve had gotten the distinct impression that Annika would have been perfectly happy to let Viktor bleed out in the street.

Brady interrupted the grim memory, asking, "How badly was your brother injured?"

"He nearly died. He was even given the last rites." She added sourly, "When Annika went to see him in the hospital, she didn't even thank him. She only wanted to know why he did it. That's when he told her he loved her. I was there." And Annika's dark gaze had merely gone narrow and calculating. As if she was thinking about ways to use his declaration to her advantage.

The man on the phone asked eagerly, "How did she react to his declaration? What did she say?"

Eve was there again in the dingy, depressing hospital room. It had been cold and rainy outside, casting dim, gloomy light on the gray-tinged sheets and too may times repainted, cast-iron bed frame. "She said she believed him. That if he was willing to die for her, it must be true."

The man on the phone replied immediately, "Her father no doubt invoked proving her love to him when he asked her to do violence as a child. The only proof of love or loyalty she'll accept involves death. She may ask Eve to die for her to prove her loyalty."

Eve jolted. "Then what will we have accomplished, other than getting me killed?"

Brady replied, "We won't let you die. I'll pull you out of the op long before I let her kill you."

"Promise?" she asked doubtfully.

"I do."

She didn't doubt that he would try to save her. But she remembered well the glint of madness in Annika's eyes. The woman was unpredictable on a good day and psychotic on a bad one. Brady might not be able to save her if Annika snapped. Of course, there was no telling what would happen if *she* snapped. The woman had practically murdered her brother. Oh, sure. Annika might not have pulled the actual trigger on the gun that killed him, but she'd darned well stood him in front of it.

Eve's gut twisted in knots of stress. She'd done her darnedest to leave that part of her life behind when she'd moved to London, the violence, the need for vengeance. She'd vowed never to deal with people like Annika or the Basque separatists again. And Brady wanted her to go back into that nightmare world?

"You don't have to do this, Eve. If it's too much for you, we'll come up with some other plan to stop her."

Every fiber of her being screamed for her to take the out. To run far, far away from this man and his mission. But then snippets of their various conversations came back to her. *I need a woman of substance and strength... You don't have what it takes to do this... Redemption... Clean slate...* A little voice in the back of her mind chimed in, whispering of revenge. Of justice for her brother. No! She'd walked away from the vicious cycle of endless violence and retaliation.

Damn him! Brady had woven his web around her strand by strand, laying down the challenge and the reward, stinging her pride, questioning the values by which she defined herself.

She looked up at him grimly. "You're very good at your job."

He didn't look too thrilled about it at the moment. "I'm sorry, Eve."

"I'm sorry, too. You've left me no choice but to go through with this even though I hate the idea more than words can express."

"You still want to do the mission, then?" he asked soberly.

Hell, no, she didn't want to do the mission. But that was no longer the question. Of all people, Eve knew exactly what kind of monster her brother's ex-lover was. If Annika was functional and on the move once more, she had to be stopped.

She gazed bleakly at the man who'd just become her handler. "I'll do it."

He reached out to push a strand of hair off her face and tuck it behind her ear with infinite gentleness. He might be sitting right there beside her, but she already felt alone. Isolated. Disconnected from everything she'd been just a few seconds ago.

She watched dispassionately as he punched a button on the phone to end the call. Then he said, "I'll take care of you. Keep you safe. You have my word of honor on it. I'll get you out of this alive."

Did she believe him? She sighed. It wasn't like she had any choice about that, either.

What had he done? Brady watched Eve in deep alarm as she withdrew before his very eyes. How bad were the scars buried in her past, anyway? She rolled onto her belly and closed her eyes as if she were napping, but tension continued to pour off of her. He'd love to know what she was thinking about, but the least he could do was respect what little privacy he'd left her.

He sat beside her, guarding her in silence, while she faked sleeping for nearly an hour. That was a long time to wallow in dark thoughts and darker memories. When her eyes finally flickered open against the glare of the sinking sun, he murmured, "Did you solve world hunger?"

She smiled reluctantly. "I wish."

"If you want to talk, I'm here. And that's a standing offer. Anytime. Anyplace." He was startled at his offer. He never involved himself in other peoples' lives—too much messy emotional baggage to deal with. And Eve's life was messier than most.

"Okay," she replied noncommittally.

He wasn't fooled. She appreciated the offer. She just wasn't ready to take him up on it. They packed up the towels and suntan lotion in the canvas bag and threw it in the back of the golf cart. The ride back to the house was quiet.

As they climbed the front steps, Eve broke the silence. "Is this place bugged?"

"Excuse me?"

"You heard me. Is the house under surveillance?"

"Not to my knowledge."

"Would you check it for cameras and microphones before supper?" she asked.

"If you'd like." He added, perplexed, "Care to tell me why?"

"I'm feeling a little too much like a bug under a microscope at the moment. It makes me a little crazy."

He suspected the day would come soon enough when she'd be grateful to know H.O.T. Watch had eyes and ears on her. But not yet. If the lady wanted her privacy tonight, she'd earned it.

When he brought out the scanner that would pick up the tiny electrical fields of surveillance equipment, Eve lifted it out of his hands and efficiently went about sweeping the living room for bugs. He supposed, given her past, he shouldn't be surprised that she knew how to use a surveillance scanner. But it still did something uncomfortable to his gut to see her acting like a trained operative. She was an innocent. A civilian. She hadn't asked for any of this. He'd forced it into her life.

With cold calculation, he'd trapped her into doing this job, and she knew it. He had no illusions about what she'd been referring to when she'd commented bitterly that he was very good at his job. She knew she'd been manipulated, but she'd realized it too late. Kicking himself for being a cad, he moved into the kitchen to begin cooking supper. He owed her one.

As they sat down to eat, he poured Eve a glass of a fine Bordeaux he'd found in the wine cooler. She startled him by shaking off her dark mood and raising her glass in a toast to him. "Here's to new beginnings."

"New beginnings," he murmured, studying her intently. "Why the sudden change of mood?"

She shrugged. "I've lived in Annika's world for most of my life. I learned long ago to find pleasure in the moment and not think much about the big picture. It's too depressing otherwise. We have tonight, you and me. I'll worry about Annika tomorrow."

It was a shockingly healthy attitude. He didn't envision her as the type to take such a wise approach to dealing with the stress of her impending mission.

"You have to quit looking at me like that, Brady. It's insulting that you're so stunned I'd take a sane attitude toward all of this."

"Sorry," he mumbled. Since when had she become a wizard at reading people's thoughts and body language? Apparently, that was yet another part of her past he'd dredged up. What other surprises did she have in store for him?

He didn't have long to wait as she commenced regaling him with hilarious stories of her childhood. Some of them included Viktor, and a few even included Annika. He was stunned that she could laugh and find bits of joy in the midst of the difficult and terrifying upbringing she'd endured. And to think that when most people looked at her, all they saw was a pretty face. They were missing the most important parts of her by far—her indomitable spirit and resilience.

The wine had been flowing freely, maybe a little too freely because he raised his glass eventually and announced, "A toast to you, Mademoiselle Dupont. Here's to that which doesn't meet the eye."

Her wineglass paused partway to her mouth. Her glowing gaze caught his in gratitude. He would never have guessed before meeting Eve that the way to a beautiful woman's heart was to compliment her mind and not her looks. Contrary creatures, women.

Eve pushed her plate back. "That was delicious. Thank you, Brady."

"You're welcome." As they stood up, he murmured, "This is your night. What would you like to do?"

"How about a walk? I'd love to see the ocean in the moonlight."

He nodded. "A walk it is."

It was a warm evening. The hike down to the beach cleared his head and left him feeling better than he had a right to. Eve seemed similarly affected, breathing deeply and smiling at the calm ocean hissing across the sand before it retreated.

She kicked off her sandals and dipped her toes in the water. "Mmm. Perfect for a swim. What do you say?"

He frowned at her. "I didn't wear swim trunks."

She laughed. "I'm not exactly wearing a bathing suit, either. But it is, in fact, anatomically possible to swim without one."

"That's not the point," he replied in growing alarm. "It wouldn't be—"

She pressed her fingers against his mouth. "If you say it wouldn't be appropriate, I'm going to have to hurt you."

He smiled against her fingertips. "Why?"

"Does anything about me or my life strike you as appropriate? I have never lived by other peoples' rules and I'm not about to start now. That's one thing Annika and I have in common."

That checked him sharply. He'd made a point of imposing

the strictest possible set of rules upon himself ever since he'd left home. He liked rules. Craved them, in fact. He wanted order in his life. A code of ethics. Honor. Hell, he didn't want what his mother had been to rub off on him. He'd been running figuratively from that for all of his adult life.

And this woman did the exact opposite. She lived by no one's rules, seizing the moment, doing what felt good, the consequences be damned. The very notion gave him a serious case of the heebie-jeebies. She embodied everything he hated in a woman.

"Don't you go all grim and serious on me, Brady," she warned him, laughingly. "I want to have fun tonight."

A shudder passed through him. Her brand of fun horrified him.

She reached for the hem of her loose gauze top and pulled it over her head all in one quick movement. She flung the garment to the sand while he tried frantically to figure out where else to look. Anywhere but at her skimpy lace bra, which he couldn't help but notice out of the corner of his eye was a push-up number she was all but spilling out the top of. The way she was stacked, she didn't need help pushing anything up.

She shimmied out of her long skirt, the white gauze pooling around her feet.

Don't look. But damned if his gaze didn't creep toward her in spite of his best effort to stop it. What man wouldn't peek when one of the most beautiful women on the planet stripped in front of him? He was only human, after all, and not dead at that.

He glimpsed her ankles as she stepped out of the circle of fabric. She turned away from him, and his gaze made the mistake of creeping upward momentarily. Oh, Lord. She had on a thong. His palms itched to cup her bare bottom, to test its firmness, to hold her still so he could—

So he could nothing. There was no end to that thought. He wasn't going to have fun of any kind with her. End of discussion.

Except Eve seemed to think the discussion was just getting going. "C'mon, Brady. Take your clothes off and skinny dip with me. I dare you."

Her hand reached for the valley between her breasts. Sweat popped out on his forehead as she snapped the front latch of her bra and it spilled open, her modesty clinging as precariously as the scraps of lace barely covering her breasts now.

"You're falling behind," Eve teased. "Have you forgotten how to work a zipper? Need me to show you how?"

The thought of her hands on his zipper made all kinds of unwelcome things happen to his body, including his breathing doubling in pace and parts of him commencing throbbing painfully, both of which he could do without, thank you very much.

Her fingers hooked under the edges of her thong and eased it over the curve of her hips and down her slender thighs. She straightened, gloriously naked and bathed in cool moonlight. He'd thought she was beautiful before, but this was in another class altogether. Mesmerized, he stared at her, the sight imprinting itself on his memory for all time.

Frantically, he pictured his mother. The way she aged before her time as a parade of men came and went. Hell, the woman should've installed a turnstile at their front door. The image made his jaw tight, but did nothing to ease his other aches.

"Here. Let me help you with your shirt." Eve stepped forward and reached for the soft fabric, pulling it up toward his head. He shoved the fabric down and stumbled back a step.

"We can't do this," he rasped.

"Why? Is there a law against swimming at night? We're the only people here. So what's the problem?"

She was *naked!* That was the problem. He didn't give in to temptation, ever. He didn't do casual flings, and he certainly didn't indulge in them with women who reminded him so much of his mother it made him faintly ill.

Not that Eve looked at all like Mona Hathaway—assuming that had actually been her name. He'd always suspected that Mona and his father had never legally been married. But the man had ponied up and put his name on Brady's birth certificate and sporadically sent Mona child support checks over the years. It was more than some men would've done.

In all fairness to Eve, her dossier didn't say anything about her jumping in and out of bed with multiple or frequent partners. Apparently, her romantic interest was reserved for military men who'd just coerced her into going on a suicide mission. Hell, she was as messed up as he was.

Her hands moved on his zipper, jolting him back to the present. He grabbed her wrists forcefully and yanked them away from him. "I don't do women," he gritted out.

"You're gay?" she asked, aghast. "No way."

"That's not what I said. I just don't do…*this.*"

"Why not? You're a man. I'm a woman. I know you're as attracted to me as I am to you. We're alone on a beautiful beach in the moonlight…" she trailed off suggestively.

"I just don't."

"I say again, why not?"

He shook his head. "I promised myself a long time ago that I would not have casual, meaningless sex with women. And I don't plan to start breaking that promise now."

She pulled back sharply. She looked offended. "Meaningless?" she repeated ominously.

"What would you call it? We've known each other, what? Less than two days?"

Her gaze narrowed to a feline glare. "Are you calling me a slut?"

"Not at all. I'm just saying I don't share your casual attitude toward sex."

She swore at him then, long and freely in French. Thankfully, he only caught a few words of it here and there. Defiantly, she marched into the ocean naked and took her swim anyway.

He had to admire her spirit. She didn't gave a damn what anyone else thought of her, and she wasn't about to live her life chasing other people's approval. He turned his back on the water when he realized he was hoping to glimpse her pale body in the black water.

He didn't care what other people thought of him, either, including Eve Dupont. No matter how tempting the woman was, he was not going to fall into the sack with her and become his mother's son.

Chapter 5

Okay, so it had been a dirty trick to strip in front of Brady. She admitted it. But she'd wanted him, and she wasn't accustomed to feeling like that around a man. Neither was she accustomed to a man turning her down.

She tossed and turned in her lonely bed for much of the night trying to figure out what his hang-up with women was about. She kept returning to that kiss they'd shared on the front porch on the night she'd arrived on the island.

He definitely wasn't gay. He'd all but eaten her alive. She'd caught him on more than one occasion eyeing her like she was some sort of edible confection. He definitely was attracted to her. And based on the innuendos he'd laced all through his training sessions with her, sex with her was on his mind. Why then had he rejected her on the beach?

What was wrong with her?

Had she not had men pursuing her as relentlessly as cats after a tender, tasty mouse pretty much from the time she'd been a prepubescent schoolgirl, the man might really give her a complex. But she had years' worth of empirical evidence to support the theory that nothing was wrong with her in the sexy and attractive department.

What, then, was wrong with him? She'd heard that some Americans could be really uptight about sex. Was that all it was? Her instinct said there was more to it than that. If he was that uptight, he wouldn't have kissed her the way he had. And she was right back to the beginning of her circular argument with herself.

Frustrated as the sun rose to end her sleepless night, and shocked at how irritable the sensation made her, she climbed out of bed. She got dressed grumpily, omitting a bra under a clingy little sweater that left her midriff bare, and donning short shorts that barely covered her behind. It was probably immature to blatantly flaunt her body after he'd refused her last night, but her ego was bruised.

She strolled out into the living room, keeping an eagle eye out for his reaction to her Barbie doll outfit. He glanced up. His gaze traveled all the way down her body and back up, and then lifted to hers. Dammit, he was back to looking at her like she was some kind of insect. An unpleasant one he'd rather squash.

She plopped down beside him on the couch and asked without preamble, "Okay. What's wrong with you?"

His right eyebrow arched sardonically. "Nothing. But thank you for asking."

She scowled. "Why don't you want to make love with me?"

"It's nothing personal. I just prefer not to indulge in that sort of thing."

"It looks to me like you don't indulge in *things* at all," she retorted. She supposed it was possible he merely had a very conservative attitude toward sex, but he watched her too

closely and his gaze burned too hot at what he saw for her
to believe that.

"You are correct that I don't do relationships for the most
part," he replied.

That stopped her cold. "Seriously?" she blurted.

He looked up from the sheaf of papers he was reading.
"Have you got a problem with that?"

His warning tone of voice made it clear she was intruding
into personal territory he didn't appreciate having invaded.
Tough. If she was going to work with him she needed to solve
this mystery.

"Why don't you allow yourself relationships?" she asked.

"I don't have time for them."

She crossed her arms, fully aware of what it did to her
cleavage, and crossed her legs, fully aware that her already
short shorts hiked even higher. He made no secret of letting
his gaze slide down to take in the sights appreciatively. This
man was *so* not a monk. She declared, "That's a cop-out. You
could make time if you wanted to."

"The right woman has never come around?" he threw out
dryly.

She snorted. "Another cop-out. You've never looked for
her, and that's different."

He leaned back, scowling. "Well then, if you know so
much about my love life or lack thereof, you tell me what's
going on."

"I don't know. That's why I asked. I'm going to fret about
this when I ought to be paying attention to Annika. I need
to know…for the sake of the mission."

One corner of his mouth quirked upward. "Nice try, but
no cigar."

She leaned forward to give him a better look down her
sweater and he didn't hesitate to take in the view. What was

up with him? Was he truly a look-but-don't-touch type? "C'mon, Brady. What have you got against women?"

"Are you hungry?" he asked grimly.

"Don't change the subject," she snapped.

"We won't be back here for several hours, so eat and drink now if you want to," he replied stubbornly. Not going to be lured into further conversation about his opinion of women, was he? Interesting. She did believe she'd struck a nerve.

"I'm not going to give up," she warned him.

"Then you're bound to be disappointed."

She played the sympathy card shamelessly. "I'm about to go to the Cayman Islands and join a terrorist cell. I'm probably going to die and I'll take your secrets to the grave with me, anyway."

He merely shrugged.

When she opened her mouth to speak again, he startled her by cutting her off with a single word. "Enough." He said the word quietly, but with sufficient bite to stop her in her tracks. It was easy to forget he was a military officer with him running around barefoot in casual jeans and T-shirts. Time to beat a tactical retreat.

Why was it she had such lousy luck with men? She couldn't stand the ones who chased her, and when she finally found a man she was actually attracted to, he wanted nothing to do with her.

She headed for the kitchen and poured herself a glass of orange juice. She chugged that, then sipped a cup of hot coffee more slowly. After she'd judged sufficient time had passed for him to calm down, she wandered cautiously into the living room.

He was standing over by the big picture window staring toward the ocean in the distance. He looked totally unreachable. She'd never known it was possible to be in the same room with someone and yet feel completely alone like this.

She chose a chair facing him and nursed her coffee while she waited for him to rejoin the living.

Finally, he turned briskly. "No more personal baggage. Just business between us. You do what I say; I keep you alive. We bring down Annika Cantori."

She nodded her acceptance of his terms, but a little voice in the back of her head asked what came after all of that. What about the two of them?

Except there was no *them*. She had to put on her big-girl panties and get over him. It was the only way she'd get a shot at redeeming herself for a crime she hadn't committed.

Chapter 6

From the air, Grand Cayman Island resembled Captain Hook's wrist, ending in a large hook. That narrow, mostly north-south hook was their destination, a strip of land and beach dominated by swanky high-rise resorts stacked next to each other like rows of dominoes. And banks. Scores of them. One of the last great tax havens on the planet, the rich and secretive flocked to the Caymans from all over the world to hide and launder their taxable assets.

It wasn't a bad place for a terrorist to hide. Privacy was a highly valued commodity on the island, and as long as a person looked affluent enough to be part of the out-of-town clientele, the locals kept their distance.

Eve scoped out the soft, white sand of Seven Mile Beach with the eyes of an expert. There was a hierarchy to beach real estate. The patrons of the hotel facing a strip of beach got dibs. But within that bunch, those who forked out for cabana service got the prime spots—far enough from the water not to get their towels wet, but close enough to be gently cooled by the breeze and salt spray. And with that location went the privilege of seeing and being seen.

She adjusted the hip strings of her barely there bikini and sauntered toward the cabana boy's stand. She flashed her room key and signed a chit charging her private clamshell shade and chaise lounge to her bill. *Thank you, Uncle Sam.* Amusement flared. How much fun was it to spend the U.S. government's money on a fabulous tan?

"Oh, and a piña colada, please," she told the cabana boy.

He smiled and left to fetch it for her.

Seven Mile beach stretched the entire length of the captain's hook. If Annika Cantori was hanging out on the resort side of Grand Cayman, she'd likely pass by here eventually.

Eve had spent most of the flight from Brady's island to this one reviewing the handful of photographs of Annika that H.O.T. Watch could come up with. A few of them had been artificially aged and had hair color and styles changed. The stack was pitifully small. But they, in addition to her having known Annika as a girl, were sufficient for Eve to be confident she'd recognize her target on sight.

Ensconced on her upholstered chaise, sipping on a cool drink and playing with its little umbrella, she languidly picked up her phone when it dinged an incoming call.

"Comfy?" Brady asked dryly.

"Couldn't be better," she replied cheerfully. "Enjoying the view?"

He cleared his throat and didn't answer the question. "Any sign of the target?"

"I've been here three minutes. Give it a little time. I thought you were the patient, disciplined one."

He didn't respond to that jibe, either. "Call me if you see anyone who could be her."

"I'll do more than call you. I'll rush up to her and give her a big, sloppy hug and gush all over her."

"I wouldn't recommend that type of approach," he blurted in quick alarm. "Her profile indicates she's extremely stingy with shows of emotion of any kind, particularly those of personal affection."

"Lighten up, Brady. She and I come from France. There's a protocol for these things. We shake hands and then air kiss each other on both cheeks. We trade small talk, agree to get together for drinks later and go our separate ways. I've got it handled."

He disconnected the call and left her to her surveillance mission in peace after that. Sunlight-soaked laziness settled into her bones as she listened to the whoosh and crash of the ocean and the murmur of voices around her.

About an hour later, her phone rang again. Half asleep, she picked it up.

Without preamble, Brady said, "H.O.T. Watch wanted me to let you know their satellite images show you're starting to burn. You might want to roll over and/or apply some more sunblock."

She burst out laughing. "Dirty little voyeurs. Tell them thank you."

She hung up the phone and pulled out a bottle of suntan lotion. Making as lascivious a production as possible out of it, she smoothed the cream over her legs and arms. She moved on to her belly and then the valley between her breasts. She took extra time there, smoothing the cream down into her cleavage and then up to her neck, across each shoulder blade, and then back down into the plunging crease between her breasts. She could just imagine the sensation she was causing among the military technicians at the other end of whatever camera they had trained on her.

She wondered what Brady thought of her little show. He

was somewhere nearby supposedly keeping a lookout for Annika with binoculars from one of the hundreds of hotel rooms fronting the beach. But she'd lay odds he was keeping an eye on her, too.

For fun, she gestured the cabana boy over, flipped over on her stomach, and popped open her bikini top. She smiled archly as the handsome teen smeared lotion all over her back. Fully aware of his potential tip, he made every bit as sexy a production out of it as she could've hoped. She didn't even say anything when his fingers dipped down her ribs, coming perilously close to the swell of her breasts.

There. That ought to keep Brady and the boys drooling for a while. She kept one eye open, idly watching the tourists strolling along the beach and reflecting on the fact that fat, tanned people were infinitely more attractive than fat, pale people.

Her phone rang again. She reached down into her beach bag and held the instrument to her ear. It was Brady's number. "Wanna have phone sex?" she purred.

"Check your ten o'clock position. Red one-piece bathing suit. Straw hat. Carrying a pair of flip-flops in her right hand. Range, eighty yards."

She sat up fast, clutching her bikini top to her chest. Not that the slack strip of cloth was doing a whole lot of good at the moment. She could barely see the figure Brady described. She reached around awkwardly to hook her suit and slipped the straps back up on her shoulders.

"If this isn't her, I'm going to be very annoyed with you," she announced. "You interrupted a perfectly lovely nap."

"You're supposed to be working, not sleeping," he retorted.

"I am working. On my tan. It's part of my cover, of course."

"Of course. Check out the lady in red. Can you identify her or eliminate her as a suspect?"

"You can really knock off all the fancy military jargon. A simple, 'Is that her or not?' would suffice."

"Fine. Is that her or not?"

"I can't tell. She'll have to get a little closer. Build's about right, though. She always did have a sort of funny-looking high waist."

"I don't care about her waist. Is it Annika?"

"Hold your horses. Her face is in shadow. I'm going to have to walk over that way to get a better look."

"Well then, get going."

"You're as impatient as a kid at Christmas. Honestly. Relax."

He snorted. "You're about to make contact with a sociopathic murderer. You could at least show a little awareness of the danger you're putting yourself into."

"Gee. Thanks." Butterflies suddenly erupted in her stomach, slamming around in there more like small, panicked birds than ethereal, nearly weightless insects.

"Good luck."

"Be quiet, Brady. You're not being any help at all, here." He was laughing when she hung up on him. She walked down to the beach and her phone rang again. Reluctantly, she picked it up.

"Let me guess. You want to me to give you a running, play-by-play commentary," she said sourly.

"That's correct. Do *not* hang up on me again."

"Grouch," she muttered. Eve strolled down toward the water and out into the shallow surf until she was about knee deep. The cool water felt like heaven on her skin after baking herself in the hot sun.

"Mmm. The water's fabulous. It's cool and refreshing on my skin. Makes me think of an ice cream cone dripping over my hand. I can just taste its sweetness and the saltiness of my hand—"

"Kill the phone sex. Just check out the target already."

Grinning, Eve passed in front of the woman in red. She glanced casually to the right, then left. She only looked directly at the woman for a second, but it was enough.

"That's her," Eve murmured into her phone. "I'm going in." She hung up the phone and stowed it saucily in the rear end of her bikini. She turned left toward her oncoming target. When they were maybe fifteen feet apart, she looked up from the surf and directly into the woman's nearly black eyes.

Recognition flared in Annika's gaze as Eve stopped dead. Stared. "Annika?"

"Eve? Eve Dupont?"

"Yes, yes, Viktor's little sister. My God. I can't believe it's you. I just assumed when Viktor died…that you had, too—how are you?" she babbled.

"I'm fine. You? What brings you here?"

They closed the remaining gap between them and did the handshake and air kiss thing exactly as she'd described it to Brady. Eve glanced at the ocean. "I came for the beach, of course, and the sun. I just had to get out of London. It was so gloomy and gray I was going to slit my wrists if I stayed there another day."

"London? What are you doing there?"

"I'm a graphic artist at an advertising firm. It's boring as hell, but it keeps the bills paid."

Annika's gaze hardened for a moment. Judging the shallow materialism of her life, was she? Eve lowered her voice. "I couldn't stay in the *Pays Basque* anymore. It reminded me too much of Viktor. Of what he stood for. Of what he sacrificed. And my mother—"

She broke off. It wasn't hard to choke up a little when she thought of her mother. "She lost the will to live. Grieved herself to death. I couldn't live in that house with her ghost and Viktor's…"

Annika nodded as if Eve had confirmed something she already knew. *Must keep tabs on the old home front.*

"So what are you up to these days, Annika? I still can't believe you're alive. It's like you disappeared from the face of the earth after…well, you know."

Annika's smiling shrug was a patent affectation. "A little of this and that. My heart was broken after your brother died."

What a load of bull. Eve made a sound of sympathy. "We should get together later. Talk some more. Drinks, maybe?"

"The Crystal Room. You know it? Eight o'clock."

She answered, "I'll find it. All right then. I'll look forward to catching up with you, Anni."

Eve thought she spied a tightening across Annika's shoulders at the old endearment Viktor used to use with her. Brady would be thrilled. The more off balance she could keep the terrorist, the better.

She returned to her chaise lounge, much satisfied with the encounter. Of course, she didn't even get to sit down before her cell phone rang.

"Report," he barked at her.

"Easy peasy," she said lightly. "I've got drinks with her at eight at someplace called the Crystal Room. We can move on to step two."

"Outstanding." He sounded genuinely pleased, and delight unfolded in her middle. To reward him for being nice, she was going to give him another backless tanning show. And this time, she was going to have the cabana boy oil up her legs, too.

Brady watched Annika until the beach curved out of sight nearly a mile beyond where Eve lay. "H.O.T. Watch, I have lost visual on the target."

"Never fear, boss," Harry Sheffield replied. "I've got her on satellite imagery." Harry was one of the top real-time photo intelligence analysis experts in the world, and one of the few men in a field dominated by women. Usually, he watched live video feeds from unmanned aerial drones flying over frontline battle targets. But he was on a forced noncombat rotation for a few months, and Brady was glad to make use of the guy's mad skills in the meantime.

"Don't lose her. We need to know everything we can about her before we send in Eve."

"We're on it," Harry replied evenly enough that Brady realized he was being gently chastised.

He sighed. His men were the best at their jobs. He didn't have to tell Harry what to do; the man would do exactly what he was supposed to without any help from an interfering boss. "Sorry," he murmured.

He swung his binoculars back toward Eve and was in time to catch the cabana boy practically groping her as the kid smeared suntan lotion all over her slim, muscular thighs. Fury flared hard and hot in Brady's gut. How dare that pimply gigolo-wannabe fondle her like that— Whoa. Stop camera. Rewind. He had no say whatsoever in who Eve did or did not let put their hands on her. She was *not* his woman.

But as her handler, he damn well could tell her to tone down the sex on the beach. He picked up the phone and started to punch her number before it dawned on him that he was reacting only slightly more civilly than a caveman here. Her life. Her body. Her damned suntan lotion. But he didn't like it. And that bothered him more than he cared to admit.

The Crystal Room was a bar at one of the more elegant resorts on the island. The crystal chandeliers from which it got its name cast sparkling prisms through the dim space. It also overflowed with potted palms that provided privacy for guests—and significant cover for guys doing surveillance on an asset's meeting with a terrorist.

He had a word with the hotel's chief of security, who was happy to let Brady slip into the bar before it opened to place several surveillance cameras in the plants. Although he planned to be in the room posing as a tourist, Brady wanted additional eyes on the meeting. Transmissions from the cameras would go directly to H.O.T. Watch headquarters.

He wasn't surprised when Annika showed up nearly a half-hour early for the meeting. The woman was dressed in a black turtleneck and tight slacks that screamed Euro-punk. Her short, spiky hair was dyed black and she wore heavy eye makeup. If he wanted to score bad drugs and kinky sex, she was the chick to hit on.

He was worried by the suspicion her early arrival for the meeting signaled. It wasn't like they could back out at this point, though. Eve was already on the terrorist's radar. Even if she didn't show up for this rendezvous, Annika would no doubt investigate Eve thoroughly. He didn't have a good read on how violent Annika would be toward the little sister of her former lover, but his best guess was that Eve was already in danger.

Eve showed up several minutes late as he'd coached her to do over the phone. He didn't want her looking too eager to speak to Annika. Not that it would ultimately allay the terrorist's suspicions. But it was the best he could do.

Every male head in the room turned when Eve walked into the bar. He fit right in watching her as she sashayed across the open space and bellied up to the mahogany bar. She wore a tight little red dress that did full justice to every sinful, curving inch of her. Even Annika seemed taken aback by Eve's smashing good looks.

Although Brady didn't dare put a microphone on Eve—and it wasn't like there was anywhere in that dress of hers to put a mic—one of the civilian technicians at H.O.T. Watch was an accomplished lip reader. She gave Brady a running commentary of the conversation between Eve and Annika.

The conversation was desultory at first, reminiscences about home and mutual acquaintances, a brief exchange of sympathy over Viktor's death. Predictably, Annika dodged the question of what she'd been up to since the cruise ship hijacking. The Frenchwoman seemed alarmed when Eve casually brought up Annika's participation in the terrorist act, and the woman's gaze skated around the room warily as if to see who might be eavesdropping.

Brady smiled into his drink. Little did she know.

They were into their third glasses of wine when Eve brought up the sixty-four-thousand-dollar question. The lip reader murmured without emotion in his ear but he could imagine Eve's breezy, casual tone. "So, Annika. Any chance you're thinking about getting back into the business?"

Annika didn't exactly spew wine all over herself, but she didn't come far from it. "And what business, exactly, would that be?" she asked sharply.

Eve smiled knowingly. "Why, the family business, of course."

Annika slammed down her wineglass and glared at Eve without any pretense of civility. "Is this a setup? Who sent you? Interpol? The FBI?" Her gaze darted around the bar anxiously. "Where are they?"

"You always were a little paranoid," Eve replied, smiling mildly. "Really. You should work on that. It draws too much attention to you, and goodness knows, that's not healthy in your line of work."

Brady held his breath. It was a dangerous gambit to bait someone as mercurial as Annika.

The Frenchwoman slugged down the rest of her glass of wine in a single angry gulp. "What the hell do you want from me?"

Eve leaned in close. "I want to pick up where Viktor left off. It took me a while to know what I want to do with my life, and I had to get the cops off my back, but my brother left unfinished business behind." She shrugged. "I'm a Dupont. It's in my blood."

Annika went utterly still.

Eve swirled her glass of wine idly and then looked over slyly at her companion. "And I know it's in your blood, too." When Annika said nothing, Eve added with a cajoling smile, "C'mon, Anni. It'll be like old times. We'll have fun."

"Fun? *Fun?*" Annika's voice rose until Brady could hear it where he was seated halfway across the bar.

Eve clearly shushed her, glancing around nervously herself. "I'm serious, Annika. I know you're active again. I want in."

Brady held his breath. The next few seconds would determine the future of the entire operation.

"How do you know such a thing?" Annika demanded.

Eve rolled her eyes. "I've got my sources. Viktor had connections, and some of them have kept in touch."

"Even if I were active again, why should I let you in?"

"You are not the only one who suffered a great tragedy. I lost my brother on that ship. For all intents and purposes, he raised me. I loved him, and they shot him down in cold blood."

"So this is about revenge?"

Eve's gaze narrowed to something angry and cold. Brady'd never seen that expression from her before. It went beyond convincing acting. That was genuine fury rolling off of her. He jolted, startled by the intensity of her reaction when she talked about her brother's death.

A new voice spoke in his ear, "Brady, it's Jennifer. Are you sure you can trust this girl? How well did you get to know her, exactly? She looks plenty steamed over her brother's death.

Is it possible she's been using you all along just to get access to Annika?"

His gut clenched in denial. He was shocked to realize he trusted her. When had that happened? "She'll come through for us," he muttered into the microphone in his collar. *He hoped.*

The lip reader continued translating. "You're talking crazy, Eve. Trust me, you don't have the stomach for what you're suggesting."

Brady didn't need a translator to read the passion pouring off of Eve. "You don't know anything about me, Annika. I've changed a lot since you disappeared. I've endured years of continuous harassment by the police, I stood aside helpless while my mother drank herself to death, and I've seen the injustices you and Viktor used to talk about with such fiery passion. I've grown up. And along the way I got cynical. Since when do you have the exclusive rights to acting upon your anger at society, anyway?"

The bartender poured Annika another glass of wine, which she sipped thoughtfully. *Don't push too hard, Eve. Easy does it.*

As if she'd heard him, Eve sat back and let her gaze roam across the room. It slid off of Brady as casually as it did every other man in the place, and a moment's pride filled him. She was a natural at this.

Annika shifted on her barstool until she was leaning so close to Eve their shoulders almost touched. And then, to Brady's dismay, she covered her mouth with her hand and murmured something to Eve.

"I can't see her mouth, sir," the lip reader announced.

Brady frowned, worried. Whatever Annika had said to Eve had put a look of dawning horror on her face. If he wasn't mistaken, Eve had paled beneath her newly acquired tan. What on earth had the terrorist just said to her?

Annika stood up and, with a sardonic smile for Eve, left the bar. Brady was torn. Should he follow Annika and see where she went, or should he stay and find out from Eve what had just transpired?

Thankfully, Harry Sheffield came onto his earpiece shortly. "We have visual on the subject. She has left the resort on a scooter, and is proceeding north along Bay Road."

Odds were Annika had someone in the bar watching Eve after her departure. Brady's money was on the bald guy glowering in the corner at no one in general. A rough fellow like that didn't fit in at a place like this.

Brady nursed his drink for several more minutes so it wouldn't appear in any way that he was following Annika before he stood up to leave. As he sauntered by Eve, he looked upward toward the ceiling briefly. He hoped she would understand the signal to join him in his hotel room.

He didn't have long to wait. He heard Eve's key card in the outer door and she slipped into the room a few minutes later.

"What did she say to you to put that look on your face?" he asked without preamble.

"She told me the only way she'd let me on to her team was for me to kill someone. Here on Grand Cayman. Some random person to prove that I'm capable of violence. I can't do it, Brady. I can't kill anyone."

'You don't have to actually kill someone. All we have to do is make it look like you killed someone and do it believably enough to fool Annika."

"Huh?"

He shrugged. "We'll fake a murder starring you as the assassin."

"I don't think I could pull something like that off," Eve replied doubtfully. "Annika's pretty smart, and she'd be really mad if she figured out that we tried to trick her."

If Annika didn't buy the act, she would be more than mad. She'd be homicidal. He answered lightly, "Then we'll have to make sure she doesn't figure it out."

"You make it sound so easy," Eve murmured.

He shrugged. "The fake kill will be easy. It's all the arrangements we have to make in advance that will be difficult, starting with convincing the Caymans police force to help us."

"Will they do it?"

Brady grinned. "I'll have Jennifer Blackfoot work her magic on them. She can talk anybody into anything."

Eve sat down on his bed, leaning against the piled pillows and stretching out her legs in front of her. The sinuous lines of her reclining body made her look like a siren out of an old movie. Desire flared low in his gut. He'd have to be dead not to react to her beauty, but still, it was a distraction he didn't need right now.

"Did she say anything else to you? Give you a deadline for this murder?" he asked.

"No. She just said I have to kill someone." Eve picked up a pillow and hugged it close enough that he might just start to get jealous of the thing. Then she asked, "Do you have anyone specific in mind for me to murder?"

"Yes," Brady answered grimly. "Me."

Chapter 7

Eve lurched up off the bed in shock more intense than when Annika'd told her to kill someone in the first place. "What? I can't murder you!" The very thought made her faintly ill.

"Glad to hear it," Brady replied wryly.

She moved across the room and spontaneously hugged him. His arms came up cautiously around her. She mumbled into the soft cotton of his shirt, "I'm serious, Brady. I could never hurt you."

He went stiff in her arms and mumbled, "Never say never. Nothing's impossible."

Like him ever relaxing around her? Or maybe him returning a bit of the monster crush she had on him?

He continued earnestly, "The day may come when you'll be more than thrilled to kill me."

"I really wish you'd quit talking like that." She buried her face in his chest and inhaled the clean, safe scent of him. He was wrong. This was a man who'd been kind to her, who listened to her, who believed in her. He was decent and honorable, even if he was far too closed off emotionally. But then, who was she to throw stones about that? At the end of the day he was a good man. No matter what he said, she could never kill him.

A finger under her chin tilted her face up to his. "You're capable of much more than you know. You can do anything you set your mind to."

Like landing him? The man in the impregnable emotional fortress? Could she get him to lower his defenses and let her in? Sadly, she doubted it. Even if she did have a special affinity for lost causes.

She followed her Gallic impulse and stood on tiptoe to kiss him. If he'd been stiff before, he went granitelike now. She smiled against his mouth. It was high time he learned he'd tangled with a woman who could give as good as she got. She didn't buy the disinterested tree imitation for one second. She continued to kiss him, ignoring his complete failure to respond.

He broke all in a rush, growling in the back of his throat as his mouth opened and he took command of the kiss. Triumphant, she ceded control of the thing to him, delighting in the desperation of his arms as he swept her up against him and crushed her to him. After the initial onslaught, his mouth gentled on hers, and she melted into their kiss, surrendering to him with an abandon that was completely unfamiliar to her. How did he do that? No other man had ever evoked such a response from her.

"You have to trust me," he murmured against her mouth. "It's the only way we'll get through this mission."

She believed him. And shockingly, she did trust him. He was the first man since Viktor whom she could honestly say that about.

She reveled in the feeling of security that washed over. It

was really nice to feel this way. She laid her head on Brady's chest and listened to his heartbeat, pounding unsteadily in her ear. He wasn't affected by kissing her, huh? Ha!

She smoothed her hands around his waist and let them drift lower toward the muscular curve of his buttocks. His heart pounded harder and her grin widened. He might talk a good talk, but Mother Nature never lied.

She vaguely heard the tinny sound of someone talking in Brady's earbud. Something about the target having a visitor.

He exhaled in what sounded suspiciously like relief and set her away from him. "I have to go." He beat a retreat so blatantly hasty it made her laugh at the door as it slammed behind him.

She looked around the hotel room speculatively. It would be in keeping with her party girl on holiday cover if she didn't return to her own room tonight. She highly doubted Annika had someone staking her room out, but Eve couldn't be one hundred percent certain of it.

Smiling broadly, she kicked off her stilettos and peeled off the tight red dress before helping herself to a shirt from Brady's closet. She crawled under the covers, snuggling into the scent of him on his pillow.

The moon had set and only darkness came in through the window when Eve woke to the feel of strong, warm arms going around her and drawing her close.

Brady spoke darkly in her ear, "Do you know what I usually do to intruders in my room?"

"Make love to them until dawn?" she murmured sleepily.

He laughed quietly. "Is something wrong, or are you here to welcome me home?"

"Welcome home, darling," she said sweetly.

He did his granite impression again, big time. Except this time he didn't thaw. He was frozen solid against her for long enough that she finally rolled over with a sigh to face him. "What's wrong?"

"Nothing," he ground out between what sounded like clenched teeth. "I like my life simple. Uncomplicated."

She tried and failed to find a context for that comment. Finally, she admitted, "I don't understand."

"Forget it."

He rolled away from her in the dark and surged out of bed. "I'll sleep on the floor."

"Whatever for? This is a king-size bed. It's plenty big enough for both of us, even if you want to hide way over on the far side so you won't touch me and my pesky girl parts."

"That's not the point. You're just—"

He broke off tantalizingly. She demanded, "I'm just what?"

He huffed. "You're tempting, all right? Are you satisfied?"

She smiled into the darkness, absolutely satisfied. Tempting was progress.

She woke up sometime after sunrise to the sound of the shower running in the bathroom. She dozed until he emerged, wearing jeans and no shirt and toweling his hair dry.

"Good morning," she murmured sleepily.

He looked down warmly at her for a moment, and then his gaze shuttered. It must have occurred to him that he was enjoying the sight of her in his bed. "Nice shirt," he commented dryly.

"I didn't think you'd mind if I borrowed it."

"As your handler, it's my job to give you whatever you need. Including the shirt off my back."

She threw back the covers and swung her bare legs out of bed. His gaze flared with satisfying heat at the sight of their tanned length. "What I could use right now from you is a little reassurance that everything's going to be all right."

He replied soberly, "Everything's going to be all right."

"That's not exactly what I had in mind by way of

reassurance." She stood up and took a step forward to bring them chest to chest.

He sighed but didn't take a step backward. "You know we can't—" he started.

"Can't and choosing not to are entirely different."

"Well, I can't," he snapped.

She gave him a wide-eyed look of dismay. "The equipment doesn't work? Well, no wonder you're so afraid of me."

"Everything works just fine," he declared irritably, "and I'm not afraid of you."

Victory. She'd provoked an emotional reaction out of him. She smiled serenely and headed for the shower. As she brushed past him, he muttered a rather unflattering epithet regarding women in general. He really was making wonderful progress in tapping into his passionate side. After all, love and hate lay side-by-side on the spectrum of strong emotions.

Brady was gone when she got out of the shower. Although she was disappointed, she took comfort from the fact that he'd felt compelled to flee before she could sashay out of his bathroom wearing only a towel.

She pulled on her clingy red dress from last night. If they were going to have more slumber parties, she would have to bring a few of her clothes over to his hotel room. Although knowing him, he'd flip out at that. He probably was right that they really should concentrate on the mission at hand. But it was darned hard to keep her mind off of him when he was so yummy.

The hotel room door opened, and she turned in quick alarm. It was Brady carrying a brown shopping bag. He smiled neutrally when he saw her. Damn. He was back to being all calm and withdrawn. "Enjoy your shower?"

"Yes, thank you," she answered. "What have you got in the bag?"

"Breakfast. I hope you like fresh tropical fruit."

"I love mangoes. I love all kinds of juicy, sweet things."

His eyes blazed briefly, but then he banked the fire in them. "Good to know."

He unpacked a smorgasbord of fruits, cheeses, bread, and bottled water. They sat down across from one another at the small table in the corner and shared the newspaper he'd purchased. She could get very used to spending time with him like this. She checked her happy train of thought, reminding herself that after this mission was done, so were they. Unless she could get through to him before it ended.

He really could use a woman in his life. Why not her? The idea of the two of them together in a real relationship was riveting. Of course, before that could happen she had to kill him. Even the idea of fake-murdering Brady made her shudder. She took a chunk of mango he held out to her on the blade of a deadly looking knife.

She asked with a sigh, "So when am I supposed to kill you?"

"The sooner the better. Annika will be impressed if you don't hesitate to kill someone. How about tonight?"

"Can you have all of the preparations done by then?" she asked in surprise.

"H.O.T. Watch has been busy overnight. They've still got a few things to take care of, but they think you can kill me tonight." He smiled wryly at her.

She reached across the table and put her hand on top of his. "If it makes you feel better, this whole murder business sounds pretty strange to me, too. I much prefer you alive."

He made eye contact with her briefly and gave her a little nod. "Thanks. Me, too." More importantly, he didn't pull his hand out from under hers immediately. The man was definitely making progress.

He asked abruptly, "Can you ride a bicycle?"

"Yes. Why?"

"That gives us a few more options. We need to do it someplace dark and relatively deserted where no bystanders will get involved and potentially get hurt."

Fear flared in her gut. "Hurt? I thought this was all going to be fake."

"It is. But Good Samaritans are unpredictable. We wouldn't want some bystander to pull a weapon and try to engage you in a shootout."

She stared at him, appalled. It was bad enough to pretend to kill *him.* No way was she going to hurt a civilian. Her misgivings about the whole stunt intensified.

"What does a bicycle have to do with all of this?" she asked.

"We're considering using a bicycle as your getaway vehicle. It's quiet and hard to trace. We'll steal a bicycle, use it for the attack, and return it to its owner before anyone knows it's been borrowed. Also, it will discourage any witness on foot from giving chase to you."

Great. People were going to be chasing her? "The police know about all of this, right? They won't shoot me on sight, will they?"

"They've been fully briefed, and Jennifer has secured their cooperation. They've offered to do anything they can to help. They'll make a point of being far away from the murder scene, but will come in with all kinds of sirens and fanfare afterward. First thing tomorrow morning, they'll launch a highly visible manhunt for you. We'll stage the shooting close enough to a surveillance camera to have bad footage of it for the police to put on TV. That should convince Annika it's real. When you fill in the details that jibe with the eyewitness footage, she shouldn't question the fact that you actually shot me."

Eve was still hung up on the first bit of what he'd said. "The police will be hunting me?"

"Of course. We have to make it look believable for Annika."

Eve shuddered. What had she gotten herself into? "Are you sure this is the only way to prove to Annika that I'm violent enough to play in her sandbox?"

"You tell me. You know her better than the rest of us. Will she accept anything shy of an actual murder as proof of your violent intent?"

"No. She doesn't do anything halfway."

Brady shrugged. "Then tonight I die."

The street they'd chosen for Brady's murder was in a business section of the capital, George Town, that was dark and deserted at this time of night. She wore black pants and a black turtleneck, her blond hair tucked up inside a black watch cap. Brady had insisted on her smearing black camouflage grease on her face and hands as well. She felt a little bit like a circus clown riding her stolen bicycle down the street.

She had a messenger bag slung over her shoulder, and the pistol inside it weighed a ton. Brady had assured her over and over that it was loaded with blanks. He'd even unloaded the weapon and shown her the dummy rounds when she continued to fret over the safety of the weapon. She'd only subsided when he reminded her dryly that he had as vested an interest as her in making sure there were no actual bullets in the gun.

Her pedaling slowed as she neared the intersection H.O.T. Watch had chosen for the murder. Her gut clenched at the mere thought of the word. She hated anything to do with harming another human being; it went against everything she'd ever stood for. The violence around her had taken far too high a toll in her life. It was not the way to solve any problem.

The alley where she would shoot Brady should be just ahead on her left. Her feet slowed, and the bike drifted forward. She looked around carefully but saw no one. They were alone. Brady would come out of that alley momentarily. He would be wearing a disguise—including a blond wig she'd insisted he model for her in his room to her peals of laughter. He'd eventually smiled reluctantly, too.

He would be carrying a briefcase in his right hand. He would check his watch on his left wrist, turn away and give her his back for the "shot," then tug on his left ear. The ear tug was the signal for her to proceed.

There he was. She wouldn't have recognized him had she not known it was him. He was dressed as a street person in a filthy T-shirt and a pair of baggy pants. He checked his watch and then he turned away from her.

Braking awkwardly, she pulled the messenger bag forward to hang down in front of her. With a last look around, seeing no one, she reached inside and grasped the weapon tightly.

Brady's left hand slipped into his pocket. No doubt to activate an exploding squib with a remote control. She been amused when the high-tech squib turned out to be a plain old condom filled with corn syrup, red food coloring, and chocolate syrup mixed to look like blood.

She could do this. It was all pretend. An elaborate game of cowboys and Indians that children might play…or Basque separatists and army soldiers, in her case.

Brady tugged his ear.

She raised her gun and was shocked to discover how badly her hand was shaking. Her palm was slick with sweat and she grasped the weapon with all her strength. Good thing she wasn't actually having to shoot him. She doubted she could hit the side of a barn right now if she tried.

She brought the bicycle to a stop and remained seated, one foot on the pavement to balance her. Remembering the powerful recoil of the pistol that had knocked her over the first time she shot a gun, she did her best to relax her arm as she squeezed the trigger.

Bang!

The sound echoed deafeningly in the concrete canyon of banks and office buildings. Brady slammed forward face-first onto the ground so convincingly she forgot for a moment that she hadn't actually shot him. A spray of something wet and red misted the air where he'd just been standing. He lay perfectly still, and a dark puddle started to spread beneath him.

Reflexive horror blanked her mind. *Oh, my God. Brady.*

Every cell in her body screamed at her to race forward. To render aid. To save him from what she'd just done to him. The bike wobbled violently and Eve had to slam her other foot to the ground to keep herself from falling over. Shaking violently, she jammed the gun into her bag. She pedaled hard, struggling with the handlebar to control the bike's shimmying as she took off. It took her several moments to regain her balance. Lord, she was a mess. She was so rattled she could hardly ride a bike.

She wheeled past where he lay unmoving on the sidewalk, and nausea tore through her gut. She never needed to see a real shooting victim as long as she lived. Racing down the street, she forced herself to concentrate on getting away from the scene of the crime without falling and killing herself. The irony was not lost on her.

Brady was maybe a half-dozen blocks behind her when the first sirens screamed in the distance. She pedaled faster. She couldn't afford to be anywhere near the murder scene when the police arrived. Not to mention H.O.T. Watch expected television crews to show up quickly thereafter.

The Caymans police had agreed to remove Brady's "body" rapidly, so he wouldn't end up starring on the evening news playing a corpse. He'd been concerned that overseas news outlets might pick up the story and that members of his family might accidentally see his "dead" face.

As prearranged, she locked the bicycle into a bike stand outside an apartment building Brady'd shown her earlier. From there she made her way to the beach, stripped off her black shirt and pants to reveal a bathing suit. After taking a quick swim to wash the grease off of her hands and face, she stuffed the clothing into her bag and made the long walk back to her hotel, just another tourist out for a midnight stroll.

The whole episode had taken under an hour, but she was utterly exhausted when she got back to her room. The emotional strain of seeing Brady fall "bleeding" on the ground had drained her much worse than she'd expected. She crawled into bed and pulled the covers up around her ears, but it didn't help the shivering that had set in.

It was fake. It was all right. Brady was fine. But she couldn't get that nightmare image of him out of her head, motionless and bleeding by her hand.

By the time she woke up the next morning, the murder was the talk of the island. It was splashed all over the news, and fuzzy images of a man pitching facedown to the ground and a brief flash of a lean figure wearing black and riding a bicycle were being shown nearly continuously on every channel. Her heart in her throat, she listened to the news coverage and was relieved to hear that the police reported having no leads or suspects in the murder.

The plan today was for Eve to return to the beach and hope that Annika would come looking for her. Even though H.O.T. Watch knew where Annika was staying, they were reluctant to make the terrorist suspicious of Eve by having her show up unannounced at Annika's front door.

Jittery, Eve made her way down to the beach and the hotel's cabanas. Within minutes her telephone beeped to indicate an incoming text message. *We have you in sight. Brady says hi and don't forget to use sunblock.*

Relief so profound it made her feel like crying rushed through her. She needed to see him, to hold him, to reassure herself that he was really alive, but the text from H.O.T. Watch was better than nothing. The plan was for Brady to stay hidden in the island's morgue until all the press went away from the place. His headquarters didn't want to take any chances with the ruse being discovered. She didn't know when she'd see him again.

Eve baked in the sun for an hour feeling horribly exposed and terrified that someone would recognize her and accuse her of being a killer at any minute. Her nerves were frayed and she was about to abandon her post when, down the beach, she spied a familiar figure. A lean woman with short black hair and wearing a red bathing suit strode down the beach purposefully. She was coming in Eve's direction.

Annika.

Here went nothing.

Chapter 8

Wearing yet another disguise, Brady left the morgue, blending in with the desultory early afternoon foot traffic and making his way back to his hotel room. Once inside, he rushed to the window to scan the beach below. No sign of Eve. He swore under his breath.

He pulled out his cell phone and dialed H.O.T. Watch quickly. "Harry, it's Brady. Where's Eve?"

"She left the beach about twenty minutes ago with Annika."

"Where did they go?" As he spoke, he changed quickly into shorts and a T-shirt that would help him blend in with the local populace.

"You can't go after her, sir. You need to keep your distance and let her do her job. If Annika's people spot you tailing Eve, not only would they be suspicious of you but they could hurt Eve."

Harry was right, dammit. Frustrated, Brady asked, "Where are they headed?"

"They appear to be en route to Annika's house. We have parabolic microphones installed across the street, and we should be able to pick up some or all of the conversation."

"Do we have infrared imagery?" Sensitive heat-detecting cameras could be pointed at a structure and literally see through the walls.

Harry responded gently, "This is an infiltration op, Commander Hathaway, not an imminent attack."

Which was a polite way of the guy saying that using infrared cameras at this juncture was neither called for nor logical. Brady sighed. He adamantly wished he were standing in the control room at H.O.T. Watch ops right now, with ready access to all of its high-tech surveillance capabilities. As it was, he was stuck in this cursed hotel room with only secondhand reports of what was going on with Eve. Impatience surged through him.

"We've got to get some sort of video monitor here in my room with whatever visuals we've got on Eve. I'm going to go crazy if I can't see more of what's happening during this mission."

Jennifer Blackfoot spoke up, "She's gotten under your skin, hasn't she?" his colleague accused.

"No, she hasn't," he protested. "I'm just worried about her. Annika's violent and unpredictable, and I worry about Eve dealing with her."

Jennifer's voice lost the faint echo of being on speaker phone. She'd come on the line to talk to him privately. She asked quietly, "Are you going to be able to hold it together, Brady? Do you need me to take over this op?"

"No, I've got it," he snapped. "I'm good."

But he wasn't good, and he damned well knew it. Moreover, Jennifer knew it. The hell of it was Jennifer knew exactly why he was such a mess, too. He had to chill out and fast, or she would go over his head and get him pulled from this op. She'd probably be right to do so, but his heart shouted in protest at the notion.

Where are you, Eve? What the hell's happening to you?

Eve was impressed when Annika made a point of walking past a police patrol on the beach. Testing Eve's nerves, was she? And not even subtly. Good thing Eve wasn't guilty of any actual crime—she never had been any good at hiding her guilt. As it was, she studiously avoided looking at the police officers for fear that one of them might show some small sign of recognition of her and blow the operation.

They passed a second patrol a few minutes later. Caymans law enforcement types were making their presence highly visible today in the wake of last night's murder. The tourists were the cash cow that kept this island afloat, and it was vital that they feel safe.

Eve said casually to Annika, "Looks like the island's finest are out in force looking for me. It makes a girl feel all warm and fuzzy inside."

Annika glanced at her sharply.

"What?" Eve asked innocently.

"You are more calm than I expected."

"First you didn't think I could do it. And now you're surprised that I'm not crying and having vapors. What kind of moron do you think I am? I'm Viktor's sister, and he was no dummy." *Although it had been pretty stupid of him to fall for a psychotic terrorist and let her talk him into getting himself killed.*

Annika conceded reluctantly, "You have his courage if nothing else."

They walked in silence after that. Annika led her to a dilapidated bungalow in what had to be the poorest section of town. The tiny yard was overgrown, and the shack hadn't seen a paint can in Eve's lifetime. They stepped inside onto bare concrete floors. Two decrepit sofas faced each other in the main room, and three rough-looking men lounged on them.

The nearest one had a shaved head and was, predictably, called Curly. The others, a pair of small, dark-haired, dark-eyed brothers named Pierre and André, grunted as Annika introduced her. The two men looked Basque and not particularly interested in her. But Eve's skin crawled at the way the bald one, Curly, undressed her with his eyes. He'd bear watching, that one.

"Eve, here, killed that guy on the news this morning," Annika announced.

Curly's gaze flickered in slightly more interest. He said in a heavy Basque accent, "I still get to make the kill, no?"

Annika rolled her eyes. "Of course."

Eve asked boldly, "Who's the target?"

Annika threw her a quelling look. "All in good time, little chick. You've barely got feathers, let alone learned how to fly."

She glared. "I killed a man last night. I'm blooded. I've earned my way in."

"You've earned *nothing*," Annika spat, "except a chance to prove yourself worthy of serving the cause."

Inside, Eve quaked at the insanity tinging Annika's voice. Total nut job, that woman was. Eve crossed her arms and struck a provocative pose. Wearing only a skimpy bikini and a nearly as skimpy cover-up, she shoved her chest up and out. "Worried about a little competition maybe?"

Annika's gaze narrowed dangerously. "Don't play with fire, little girl. You'll burn to death."

Eve turned and headed for the door speaking over her shoulder in disgust. "I'm out of here. When you can treat me like the adult I am, we'll talk. Until then…" she uttered a foul epithet in French describing what Annika could do with herself.

The men burst out laughing, startling Eve badly. She reached for the doorknob and prayed no one noticed how her hands were shaking.

"Wait," Annika said in a conciliatory tone.

Eve turned around slowly. "Who's the target?"

"Someone important. More important than you can imagine. He's rumored to be coming here for a series of secret meetings very soon. And I've got a job for you. You're the perfect person for it."

Eve moved back into the room trying to feign an eagerness she was far from feeling. "Anything. What can I do?"

"Sit on a beach and look useless," Annika announced.

"I beg your pardon?" Eve was puzzled.

"There's a resort—the Three Palms. Very exclusive. Very high end. I need you to get onto its private beach and hang out there. Watch who comes and goes and report back to me. When our target arrives, you'll let me know."

"How am I going to spot the target if I don't know who he is?" Eve asked.

"Oh, you'll know who he is when he arrives," Annika replied, smiling like a shark on the hunt. The expression sent a chill down Eve's spine.

"How do you want me to stay in touch? Cell phone? Email? Dead drop?"

Annika rolled her eyes. "I'll contact you when I want an update. Until then, do what you do best. Blend in with the beautiful people and keep your eyes open. I'll be in touch."

Eve nodded thoughtfully. A male target. VIP. Inbound to the Three Palms soon. She stepped outside and was startled when a trio of youths whistled and made bald suggestions to her about what they'd like to do with her. She laughed as if they were cute and she would actually contemplate taking them up on their various raw offers in this lifetime. *Not.*

The Three Palms, huh? It was an incredibly exclusive resort. The obvious approach, likely the one Annika expected her to take, was to pose as a high-priced call girl canvassing the joint for business. Small problem: a place like the Three Palms would take a very dim view of working girls prowling their beach.

She headed back to her hotel, turning over various plans for getting onto the private beach and being allowed to stay there for the hours or days it would take to stake out this VIP target of Annika's.

Eve realized she'd stopped in front of Brady's door on the tenth floor of their hotel and not her own on the sixth. He'd had their rooms keyed so their key cards worked in either door. She put hers in the lock now and stepped inside.

Brady turned away from the window and stepped forward wordlessly to take her in his arms. She buried her face against his neck and hung on for dear life, while he buried his face in her hair and did the same. The last time she'd seen him he'd been lying facedown in a pool of fake blood. The impact of seeing him alive and well once more was staggering. It took her a minute to register in shock that he'd initiated this contact. Would wonders never cease?

"Thank God you're alive," she breathed.

He murmured back, "Thank God you're safe."

"I'm never shooting you again, fake or otherwise."

He laughed quietly. "Never say never. You did great."

"I was so scared I could barely pull the trigger."

"But you did do it. I'm proud of you."

Warmth started in her tummy and spread all the way to her toes.

"Tell me about your meeting with Annika."

He led her over to the armchairs by the window. She

ignored the second chair and sank down into his lap. To her mild surprise, he didn't dump her on the floor. In fact, he only looked uncomfortable for a few moments. Although he did seem to be having a terrible time trying to figure out what to do with his hands. He settled for plastering his palms on the arms of the chair.

"She took me to her house and introduced me to three men. I can sketch them for you later. She was rude to me at first, but I think it was a test. When I threatened to walk out on her, she backed down."

"Did she give you any idea what she's planning?"

"She told me to go to the Three Palms resort, and watch for a target to show up. She refused to tell me who he is but said he's important and I'll recognize him when he arrives."

"So it's an assassination then."

"That's definitely my impression. One of the guys, Curly, was worried that he wouldn't get to be the shooter if I was brought on to the team."

His left arm went lightly around her waist to prevent her from getting out of his lap while he leaned to one side and dug his cell phone out of his pocket. She laid her head on his chest as he spoke into the phone. "You got all that on the parabolic mics? That's right. Three Palms. A male VIP who's arriving soon." A pause, then, "I'll let you know." He disconnected.

"What are you supposed to let them know?" she asked.

"If you give me any additional information."

"Like the fact that I don't think I can do this alone, and I don't know how to get into the Three Palms without being arrested? Or the bit where I'm frantically trying to figure out how you can be there with me plausibly?"

His arm tightened around her. "I don't think I can do this apart from you, either," he confessed.

She froze. Raised her head to stare at him. "Really?"

Pleasure raced through her like wildfire at the notion that

he couldn't stand being separated from her. Either that or he was just terrified she'd screw up the mission. She put her hands on his face and leaned forward to kiss him. She probably shouldn't, but she couldn't help herself.

He made a halfhearted effort to stop the kiss, but in a matter of seconds he met her halfway. How she ended up straddling his hips with her cover-up bunched up around her waist she wasn't quite sure. She just knew she had to get closer to him. Break through that damned reserve of his to connect with the man beneath.

How was it that someone so determined to keep his distance from her made her feel whole in a way that no one else ever had? It was crazy. She was crazy. Maybe she felt safe with him precisely because he was unattainable. The backward logic was messed up, but then she'd never pretended to be normal or well-adjusted.

His desire to be with her might be a temporary thing fueled by his fear and stress, but it was enough. For now. A tiny voice in her skull warned that it might not always be enough, though. If she knew what was good for her, she'd stop this madness and give up on him.

But when had she ever done what was good for her? What sane person volunteered to infiltrate a terrorist cell led by someone who'd kill her if she stepped even a millimeter out of line?

He pulled back reluctantly and muttered in open annoyance, "I can't seem to get enough of you."

"That's wonderful," she smiled.

"Speak for yourself," he grumbled.

She laughed and kissed him again. "When will you realize you're a lost cause and stop fighting this thing between us?"

He stared at her in horror. And then he did all but dump her onto the floor as he surged out from beneath her. He turned grimly to face her. "I'll find a way to be at the resort with you. But this thing between us ends here."

She just shook her head. He was fighting himself so terribly hard. When would he take an honest look inside his heart and see his feelings? She only hoped he got around to it before Annika killed her.

Brady knew better than to kiss Eve. But he couldn't find it in his heart to give a damn that he had. Just like he knew better than to make himself a visible part of the mission. And yet, as sure as he was standing here, that was exactly what he was going to do. Eve wanted him with her, and so it would be.

Jennifer Blackfoot was going to have a cow.

He and Eve both started when his cell phone rang abruptly. It had fallen down between the cushions of the chair, and the two of them laughed as he frantically dug it out.

"Go," he said shortly.

It was Jennifer. "We've searched the government database for scheduled movements of various world leaders to the Three Palms resort and come up empty. A preliminary search of announced business executive and celebrity movements is also a bust. We need to find out from the manager of the resort who has reservations there over the next several weeks."

"Will do. Eve and I will work out an excuse for her to hang out at the resort."

"How's she doing after her encounter with Annika?"

"A little shaken, but she seems to be doing better." He smiled at Eve, who gave him a dazzling response. She lit up the entire room when she smiled like that.

"We'll have a transcript of the conversation our microphones picked up for you momentarily. I'll email it to you, Brady."

"Thanks. Anything else?"

"Tell Eve she did well. I was worried when she confronted Annika so forcefully, but her instincts were good."

Brady disconnected the call. "What's this about you confronting Annika forcefully?"

Eve winced fractionally. "Well, she can be a bit of a bully. I remembered Viktor saying once that to gain Annika's respect you have to push back against her sometimes. So I did."

"Just be careful. Don't underestimate her, and don't ever forget you're dealing with a killer."

"I think she's worse than a killer. I think she's a genuine sociopath. Not only does she kill, she feels nothing when she does it."

Brady nodded soberly. "That would also mean loyalty or friendship from her is superficial at best. Never trust her, and never forget who you are dealing with. You'll have to stay on your toes around her at all times."

If only he could do this operation for Eve, he would. He had dealt with Annika's type before. It took a delicate touch and deft observational skills, both of which had taken him years to perfect. Eve wasn't even remotely prepared to cope with the woman. Fear clenched his gut until it cramped painfully.

"When are you supposed to meet with Annika again?"

Eve frowned. "She said she would find me. She gave me no contact information whatsoever. No cell phone number, no email address, nothing."

Damn. Annika still didn't trust Eve. Which meant she still might kill Eve at the slightest provocation. It also meant that Annika was probably not done testing Eve. He swore under his breath.

"What's wrong?" Eve asked. She was good at reading him and had picked up on his sudden tension.

"Annika's going to pull something else with you. I don't

know what. Perhaps she will want you to commit some other crime. Or maybe she's planning to do something to you. Either way, I don't like it."

"It doesn't really matter," Eve shrugged. "Whatever it is, I'll just have to get through it. After all, I'm already partway in to her gang. It would be ridiculous for me to quit now."

"It would be even more ridiculous for you to die," he snapped.

"I'll be okay, Brady. I can handle whatever she throws at me."

He shook his head. "I'm not so sure about that. Annika is genuinely psychotic. You have no idea how dangerous she truly is."

"She made a terrorist out of my brother and got him killed. She's responsible for the deaths of dozens or even hundreds of innocent civilians. And I know she wouldn't hesitate to kill me. What more do I need to know?"

He hugged her tightly and wished desperately that there was some way to wrap her in a protective shell and keep her safe. But he, of all people, knew that true safety in this world was an illusion. He'd seen more death in his career than Eve could begin to fathom, and he'd personally been the cause of some of it.

"Just promise me you'll be careful around her," he mumbled into her hair.

Eve laughed. "I definitely promise that."

She had to stay alive for him—the thought stopped him cold. *For him?*

He'd be in deep trouble if anyone got wind of just how attached he was becoming to Eve. He'd been chosen for this mission specifically because of his ability to hold himself apart emotionally, particularly from beautiful, vulnerable women. He was well on his way to spectacularly blowing this op.

"What's next?" she asked.

"We have to get you over to the Three Palms and establish a cover. Did Annika suggest anything?"

"No. I imagine she sees me posing as a prostitute and working the customers."

His arms tightened involuntarily around her. "No," he said flatly.

She shrugged. "I'm not freaked out at posing as a working girl. Some people think I must be a pro because of how I look. I know how to fend off the…monetary propositions."

"What you need is a ring on your left ring finger," he growled.

She laughed. "Are you planning on putting one there?"

He jolted. Marriage? Him? Not in the cards anytime soon, thank you very much. Not with his job. He dedicated himself one hundred percent to his career, and until that changed, no way did he have the time or emotional wherewithal to do any woman justice.

He shrugged. "If I were you, I'd buy a gold band and wear it to keep men from bugging you."

"I doubt a ring by itself would do the trick. I'd probably need a big, angry husband hovering nearby to make the threat work."

"It sucks being beautiful, doesn't it?" he commiserated.

"There are times when it absolutely does." But then she added reflectively, "But at other times, like when I'm with you, I'm glad I'm appealing to you."

Appealing? The woman was downright addictive.

"How do you feel about being my mistress?"

She blinked, clearly startled. "Hmm. I hadn't thought about that. But, I guess…yes. I could do that."

His heart leaped. Did she think he was proposing that for real? The idea of having her as his woman, anytime he wanted to be with her, of having her waiting for him whenever he came home—it galvanized him. Surely she wouldn't agree to such a thing. She knew he was talking about the mission. Right?

He continued, "I could pose as a businessman staying at the Three Palms. We could meet and I could set you up in your own room as my mistress. Annika could approach you easily that way, but you could also be seen with me. It would give you a big, angry man at your side to keep away the jerks."

She looked crestfallen.

Something in his chest heated and expanded. She had thought his offer was a real one. And she'd still accepted it. Fierce possessiveness surged through him. Oh, yes, a big, angry man, indeed. A big protective man who would be keeping an eagle eye on her.

"That could work," Eve replied. "And I'd be glad for the backup. Annika's men are really scary."

"They didn't threaten you in any way, did they?" he asked quickly.

"Not at all. Just the usual undressing me with their eyes stuff."

His jaw clenched. He'd watched his men go all Neanderthal in the field before over women, and he'd always told them to cool it. To keep their heads in the game. And they'd always ignored him. In a flash of clarity, he finally understood why.

He ground out, "I'll call the Three Palms. Make the arrangements. And I'll also be having a word with their manager and chief of security. You'll have all the backup you need if Annika tries to pull something with you." *More like* when *Annika pulled something with her.*

Eve nodded sleepily. She'd had a few big days in a row. He stretched out on the bed and was gratified when she promptly snuggled up beside him. He murmured, "Close your eyes. I've got you now. You're safe."

She drifted off, and he savored the trusting way she nestled against his side. He didn't know what they were building between them, but it was good, whatever it was. Now, if only Jennifer Blackfoot would see it that way.

He napped and she slept until the sun had set and evening was settling over the island. They might have slept longer, but Eve's cell phone rang, startling Brady from pleasant dreams of life with Eve as his mistress.

She fumbled at the phone and got it to her ear on the third ring. "Hello?"

As she listened, dismay blossomed across her features. "Sure. I'll be there right away. Fifteen minutes." She closed the phone and looked up at him, her eyes wide and worried. "Annika wants to see me. Now."

Chapter 9

The bar Annika chose for their meeting turned out to be less than three blocks from where Eve had shot Brady the night before. Surely that was no coincidence.

"I'll go with you," Brady declared.

Eve sighed. "You know you can't. Annika will have her crew there and one of them might spot you. They'd recognize you at the Three Palms."

"But we've got no surveillance set up for this meeting," he protested.

"Then I guess I'll have to do my job and go in all by myself."

"I don't like it."

She smiled to lighten the mood, but the truth was she didn't like it, either. She didn't have any choice, though. Right now, what Annika wanted, Annika got.

"I'm going to put a bug in your purse." Brady raised a hand to forestall any arguments from her. "It's inside an MP3 player and looks exactly like the guts of the radio. It would take a microscope to tell it from the real thing. Annika can tear your player apart and still not know she's looking at a bug. It even plays music."

She took the player and its jumble of earplugs and stuffed it in her purse without argument. She might be walking a tightrope, but she wasn't quite ready to do it without a net.

The seedy bar was a far cry from the Crystal Room of two nights before. As Eve looked around the smoky interior, she was grateful she'd dressed down. Not that jeans and a baggy T-shirt prevented the usual whistles and catcalls.

Annika was seated in a booth in the far corner, her back against the wall just like the old gunfighters in American Western movies, wearing her usual Goth attire. Eve slid into the booth beside Curly. There was no sign of Pierre or André, but surely they were nearby.

She glanced down at the empty table in front of Annika. "You're not drinking tonight?"

The terrorist shrugged. "I was just waiting for you."

Alarm was as sharp and bright in Eve's throat as a dagger to the windpipe. "Are we going somewhere?"

"Yes. Let's go."

It was another test. Eve was sure of it. Probing to figure out what Annika was up to, she asked lightly, "Are you going to show me how to do something cool like wire—"

Annika cut her off with a violent slash of her hand through the air. "Never talk about such things, even in jest. It draws attention. Makes people remember your face. Surely Viktor taught you that."

Eve laughed to hide her nervousness. "Not an issue for me. People remember my face regardless of what I do."

Annika gave her a sour look. "I'll bet they do. Normally, I wouldn't use you on a team for that very reason. But in this case, I can use your looks to get into that resort. Assuming you're alive in an hour."

Eve sighed. "Do you threaten all your new recruits like this? Because really, it's getting old. Kill me or accept me, but just get on with it."

Annika's gaze went black. Opaque. Hard. *Yikes.* The psycho terrorist was back in full force. Eve slid out of the booth and followed the woman from the bar. Curly fell in behind them. Worried she might make a break for it, were they?

As they strode toward the part of town where Eve had shot Brady, she asked more cautiously, "So where are we going?"

."You talk too much. Your brother used to say you were a chatterbox. I see what he meant."

Viktor thought her chattering was cute. He said so himself. She wasn't going to let Annika's cruelty sully the memory of him laughing at her when she'd recount every detail of her day to him at ninety miles per hour.

As they walked, Eve caught a tiny movement that made her blood run cold. Annika's right hand brushed over the bulge under her black leather jacket at her right hip. The woman had a weapon holstered there and had just unconsciously touched it.

Eve debated whether or not to mention the weapon for the sake of the bug in her purse, but decided against it. Brady would assume Annika was armed, or at least not be surprised to learn she was. It wasn't worth risking her cover to say anything.

Annika's steps slowed. Eve glanced around and recognized the corner Brady had been standing on when she shot him. Her heart in her throat, she muttered, "I thought smart criminals don't return to the scene of the crime. Isn't that only for amateurs?"

The other woman pursed her lips. "I saw that film of the

shooting on TV and it didn't look quite right. I've shot a number of people, and that guy you killed fell down funny. Show me again where you were in relation to him when you shot him?"

What was her game? Eve tried frantically to figure out where Annika was going with this, but she hadn't a clue. And worse, she didn't know the first thing about crime scene forensics to fake her way through this conversation. Her best bet was to stick with the truth.

Eve looked around and pointed. "I was over there. I came from that direction. When I spotted that man by himself on the corner, he was the perfect target. Alone, standing in a shadow. Not too prosperous looking." She glanced around. "And there are about a million exit routes from here. I figured if someone spotted me they'd have a hell of a time following me for long."

"The bicycle was clever," Annika allowed. "It gave you speed over anyone pursuing you on foot, and maneuverability over any car that might have chased you."

Eve nodded, grateful for Brady's cleverness. Lord knew she would never have thought of such a thing on her own.

"What kind of gun did you use?" Annika demanded.

"A .38 revolver. Smith and Wesson." Which was about the sum total she could tell Annika of the gun.

"Did you steal it?"

"No. I bought it from a guy I found on the internet."

"Do you still have it?"

Crap. Was she supposed to dump the thing in the ocean or something? Aloud, Eve snorted. "Of course I do. It's hard to get a decent gun on an island like this. And why try to get rid of the thing and chance the police finding it and linking it to the murder?"

Annika grinned. Apparently, that had been the right answer. Eve mentally sagged in relief. She listened surreptitiously as

Annika's cell phone rang, and the terrorist spoke in rapid Basque. It was an incredibly old and difficult language to master, and Eve's father had not been a native speaker of it. But she hadn't grown up in the Pyrenees for nothing. She picked up enough to know that someone had just told Annika the person being watched had left the building.

"We're not going to do your assassination right now, are we?" Eve gasped.

"What assassination?" Annika demanded sharply.

"Oh, come now," she replied. "You want me to watch a swanky resort for an important man, and Curly asks if he still gets to take the shot? You're planning to kill someone."

Annika said nothing. She merely took off walking rapidly down the sidewalk, leaving Eve behind. Curly caught up to Eve and took her roughly by the upper arm to hustle her along.

She glared at the big man and shook off his hand. "Touch me again, buddy, and you'll withdraw a bloody stump."

Curly scowled and Annika laughed, commenting, "The kitten's got claws, eh?"

Eve winced. The dirty look Curly was giving her promised retribution later, when the boss lady wasn't around. She probably should've kept her big mouth shut, but guys like him who thought they could push around women made her mad.

Annika stopped without warning and turned to Eve. "How are you at breaking and entering?"

"I beg your pardon?" Eve asked blankly.

Annika snorted. "Some terrorist you are. We're going to break into this building. Watch and learn."

Eve looked up sharply. "The criminal justice center? Why? What's in here?"

"The morgue," Annika replied.

The—holy mother of God. Annika wanted to have a look

at the body of the man Eve had "killed." Except there was no body. *Now* what was she supposed to do? She looked left and right. Should she make a run for it? A few cars cruised past, but did she dare stake her life on one of them stopping if she flagged it down? Besides, she'd never outrun Annika's bullets.

While she frantically tried to come up with options, Annika led the way around the building to what appeared to be an employee parking lot. Pierre and André materialized out of the shadows.

"Simple locks and a number keypad," Pierre muttered. "André watched with binoculars and got the combination someone used on the number pad. All we have to do is pick the lock and we're in."

"Do it," Annika ordered.

Eve fidgeted. "Do we really have to go into a morgue? I don't like dead bodies."

"Don't be squeamish," Annika replied scornfully. "If you can put a bullet in someone, you should at least be able to look at him afterward."

How was she supposed to explain the missing corpse? Eve broke into a steady stream of mental swearing in French. It wasn't productive, but she didn't know what else to do. Her only chance was to brazen this out. Play dumb. Suggest that maybe the police had sent the body elsewhere for a more detailed autopsy. What would Brady tell her to do right now? Run for it? Lie? Make up something? But what? If only he could signal her! All too quickly, the heavy door swung open.

"After you," Annika said silkily.

Great. The crazed terrorist with the gun was now at her back. André led the way down a darkened hall. Eve was so jumpy she could hardly breathe. There was another lock on the stainless steel doors leading to the morgue, but this one André merely smashed through with the butt of a sawed off shotgun he pulled from under his long raincoat. Eve flinched as the crashing noise of splintering plastic and metal echoed through the hall.

André, Pierre and Annika hurried inside, but Eve couldn't make her feet carry her forward. Her survival instinct simply wouldn't cooperate with this madness. Curly gave her a hard shove, though, and she had no choice but to stagger into the morgue. She hissed a foul name at him over her shoulder in French.

Annika laughed. "Watch out for him. He likes to teach his women manners the hard way."

Eve snorted with false bravado to cover how she was shaking from head to foot, "I'll never be his woman."

Annika shrugged. "He's not in the habit of asking permission."

Eve's momentary irritation at Curly pushed back her fight-or-flight panic for just long enough that she didn't bolt screaming as Annika strode over to the long wall of square metal locker doors and opened the first one. Methodically, the woman opened refrigerated units. Thankfully, most of them were empty. But a few held human forms covered in white sheets.

Eve all but fainted as Annika threw the first sheet back to reveal a dead woman. That was going to be her in a few minutes. Eve announced, "We ought to have a lookout after all that noise André made. I'm going to wait outside."

Annika whirled so fast Eve barely saw her turn and pull her gun. She jammed it up against Eve's left cheek as Curly lunged and grabbed her from behind. Eve's blood ran cold when she saw the glazed look in Annika's eyes. Monsieur Cantori used to get that exact same look just before he beat the crap out of someone.

"What are you so worried about, little kitten?"

"I t-told you. I don't l-like dead b-bodies," Eve stammered. Lord, her legs felt like jelly.

"Time to get over it. You open the next door."

Eve shook her head, but the pistol barrel jammed even harder into her face. "Do it," Annika bit out viciously. Then she added in a growl that sent shivers down Eve's spine, "You don't think I'd let you die fast, do you? Can you imagine what the boys will do to you if I let them?"

The woman was insane. Completely certifiable. Eve trembled from head to foot. *Save me, Brady!* A vision of his handsome face swam before her eyes. Dammit, she'd really wanted to get together with him before she died. She was convinced they could have something special if he would just let go of his attitude about women. And Annika was going to cost them that chance.

Deep within her panic, something snapped inside Eve's head. It was as if she went a little crazy herself. She wasn't going down without a fight. Brady deserved better from her than that.

"I don't know what the hell's wrong with you, Annika. This isn't a game. Do you have any idea how hard it was to find you? I had to bust my behind and lie to all kinds of government officials to get to you. I don't need all these stupid tests of yours to prove myself. The fact that I'm here says it all. Now why don't you put down that gun? Let's get out of here before that lock André smashed brings the police down on our heads."

"I'm not leaving until I see this victim of yours," Annika snarled. But the madness retreated a tiny bit from her eyes.

Curly gave Eve a push toward the remaining refrigerated drawers. She might have bought herself a reprieve, but the cold, hard circle of Annika's pistol pressed painfully into the middle of her back now. Eve forced herself to open the heavy stainless door.

"Pull out the shelf," Annika ordered, giving her a good jab with the pistol.

Eve did as she was told and, squeezing her eyes tightly shut, threw back the sheet. She was helping Brady stop this psychopath. She concentrated on picturing him, and renewed strength of purpose flowed through her. Together, they were going to stop this woman for good.

She jolted as Annika's body pressed sickeningly against her back, the gun moving to the side of her neck. "Look at him," Annika demanded in Eve's ear.

Eve pried her eyelids open. Nausea rolled through her at the sight of a dead teen, a boy of maybe sixteen and far too skinny to be mistaken for Brady. "That's not him," she choked out.

Annika pushed her to the next row of drawers, crooning, "Show me your kill, little kitten. I'm waiting."

The woman's comments grew steadily more erratic and disjointed as Eve opened the next compartment and the next. The wilder the woman got, the more terrified Eve became. If she used the bug in her purse to beg Brady to save her, he would never get here in time. She was on her own to brazen this out and manage Annika's violent temper as best she could.

She threw the last door open. Empty. Annika pressed the gun against Eve's temple. The terrorist's head tilted back slightly and the whites of her eyes showed maniacally. "You lied to me? You *lied to me?*" Annika's voice rose to a screech.

She had to get out of here. Away from Annika. An urge to sprint for the door nearly overcame her. Must distract the crazy woman with the gun first. She glanced frantically over Annika's shoulder. "The tables," she gasped. "We haven't checked those."

Annika strode over to the first operating table. She flung back the sheet and Eve's knees nearly collapsed out from under her. A man in his thirties, of a similar height and build to Brady, lay stretched out on the table. His neck was propped on a wooden block and part of his skull had been shaved to reveal an ugly red hole in the back of his head behind his left ear.

She was not a particularly religious person, but an abject prayer of thanks came to her mind. "That's him," Eve announced in profound relief.

Annika grabbed the corpse's remaining hair and lifted his head to examine the bullet wound. She let the head drop with a dull thud. "Well, well. The kitten did it, after all. I truly didn't think you had it in you."

Eve merely shrugged. She wasn't about to push her luck and say anything to provoke Annika. She'd obviously been working herself up to killing Eve, and instinct screamed that the woman was still in a dangerous mental state. Annika would attack on a hair trigger provocation right now.

"Let's get out of here. This place stinks," Annika announced.

Eve was first out of the room on wobbly knees. The door across the hall rattled as she raced by, startling her badly. She put on a burst of speed and sprinted from the building. A vague sense of triumph registered in her gut. She'd done it. She'd overcome her fear and survived the crisis. *But not by much,* her more reasonable self whispered.

She was in. Annika believed her. She'd successfully infiltrated a dangerous terrorist cell. Now all she had to do was take it down from the inside. No sweat, right?

Brady mopped the sweat off his forehead with one hand and painfully unclenched his fingers from the hard case of his cell phone. *Good Lord, that had been close.*

He'd wanted desperately to tell Eve to play out the scenario, that H.O.T. Watch had matched his clothing and physical description to a corpse they'd shipped in from Jamaica precisely because it had been similar in size and build to Brady. But he'd had no way to communicate with her.

The unidentified man in the morgue had been dead a few weeks, but Annika wasn't likely to realize that at a glance. The experts at H.O.T. Watch had even set up Brady's fake shooting—the direction and angle Eve approached him from—to mimic John Doe's head wound.

Brady'd thought it had been overkill, but Jennifer Blackfoot had insisted on the extra precautions. She'd been worried about leaks to the press or something exactly like Annika's break-in to the morgue. God bless his colleague's paranoia. It had just saved Eve's life. Not to mention, it might have ensured the success of the entire operation.

"Thanks, Jenn," he muttered into his cell phone.

"You're welcome. This Annika chick is some piece of work, huh?"

"Don't remind me," he retorted sourly. He was more tempted than he cared to admit to pull Eve out of the whole thing. He'd take her back to that island for a couple of weeks and keep her all to himself. Funny how, as her handler, he was supposed to talk her out of chickening out, but she was the one barreling full steam ahead, and he was the one having to talk himself out of bailing on the mission.

His alarm didn't lessen when Annika took Eve back to the cell's bungalow across town. Now that Eve was officially part of the group, apparently Annika wanted to keep her close by at all times.

He didn't care what Jennifer Blackfoot said. He wasn't sitting around this hotel room miles away from Eve, twiddling his thumbs while she sank or swam alone. He had to get close to her. Close enough to rescue her himself if she needed it.

Jennifer wasn't going to like it. In effect, he would become a field operative as well, doubling the size of the mission and invoking all the attendant dangers of it upon himself. She would just have to get over it because the matter wasn't open for discussion. He was moving in close to Eve come hell or high water.

Chapter 10

The hotel's elevator door closed behind Eve and she pulled out her cell phone quickly. She had only a few moments to contact Brady. Pierre was waiting for her in the lobby, and he would expect her back downstairs with her luggage soon.

In an effort to buy herself a little more time, she'd told him she still had to pack her things. He'd grumbled about amateurs not staying ready to move on short notice and she'd laughed, assuring him that she was definitely an amateur at this gig.

She desperately needed to see Brady, if only to reassure herself that she was all right, that he didn't hear anything in Annika's voice to indicate she still planned to kill Eve.

"Go ahead," Brady said tersely as he answered his phone.

"Hi. It's me."

"Where are you? Is it safe for you to talk?"

"I'm in the hotel. In an elevator. I'm on my way up to my

room to collect my things and check out. Annika wants me to move in with her."

"You're alone?"

"Yes. I convinced Pierre to wait for me in the lobby."

"I'll be in your room in sixty seconds," he replied immediately.

Thank God.

True to his word, he burst into her room about ten seconds after she got there. He was breathing hard. Must have sprinted down the four flights of floors separating their rooms. Without saying a word, he strode forward and wrapped her in a crushing bear hug.

She inhaled the smell of his aftershave, letting it wash over her and through her, masculine, spicy and infinitely comforting. Her leftover terror from the encounter with Annika in the morgue faded before the immediacy of his embrace. She'd survived. It had turned out all right. Everything would be fine.

He seemed to know she needed to absorb some of his strength, and he gave it to her freely. She let his confidence and calm infuse her. He had her back. An entire team of experts was observing and listening to her every move. They and Brady wouldn't let anything bad happen to her.

But she still had to ask, "How close did I come to dying in the morgue?"

His arms tightened around her. "A SWAT team was in the hallway outside. A sniper had his gun trained on Annika. He'd have shot her through the wall with a single word from me.

"You mean I was scared out of my mind for nothing?"

"Just because the shooter was there didn't mean he could necessarily have taken her out before she shot." He added reluctantly, "You were in plenty of danger."

She shuddered against the solid, warm wall of his body.

"I've got you," he murmured. "You're safe. You shouldn't ever be in that kind of danger again as long as you don't do something to send Annika into orbit."

She burrowed closer to him. And then a random thought made her lift her head. "How did the SWAT team get out of that hallway when we ran out of the morgue?"

Brady chuckled. "It was a close thing. They had to scramble into the room across the hall. Barely got the door closed before you all came flying out of there. It would have been funny as hell if we weren't all holding our breaths that Annika might have spotted them."

She laughed. "I thought I saw that door move."

"The guys will be annoyed to hear you saw that."

"Will there be someone close by Annika's house to rescue me if she goes nuts?"

"Absolutely," Brady declared. "Me, for one. There'll probably be an audio/visual technician or two, as well. If things look like they're starting to get dicey, I'll call the local police and make sure they're close, too. From here on out, we'll have a safety net around you at all times."

"Won't you have to sleep now and then?"

"Now and then. I'll rest when Annika does." He asked reluctantly, "How long do you have to pack?"

She shrugged. "As long as it takes. But Pierre's not a guy I want to make mad. Of the three men in the group, he seems to dislike me the least."

"Would you consider him an ally?" Brady asked with interest.

"I wouldn't go that far. He's not an active enemy, and that's more than I can say for Curly. That guy really seems to hate me."

With a sigh, she stepped out of his arms and laid her empty suitcase on the bed. She started opening drawers and lifting their contents into the luggage.

Brady commented, "Curly probably resents your beauty. He knows he doesn't stand a chance with you, and it pisses him off to see something so desirable yet so unattainable."

She looked up at him and grinned. "Or maybe he just despises women."

"He wouldn't work for Annika if he truly did."

"Not unless he likes killing people more than he hates girls."

Brady sighed. He seemed unhappy at the reminder of how violent the people were with whom she was working. "She's going to want to establish her authority over you. Don't pick any fights with her for now, okay? Just go along with the program and try not to make waves."

"Got it," she said in a muffled voice from inside the closet.

He continued urgently, "They're all going to be trying to figure out where you fit on the team. Your best bet is to convince them you're happy to hang out at the bottom of the pecking order."

He sounded so concerned it kind of made a girl feel special. She smiled at him as she dumped her clothes in the suitcase. "All right. I won't make trouble."

He nodded, looking relieved. "H.O.T. Watch has a Basque translator on his way to the facility. By tomorrow, we'll be able to understand everything Annika says. Does she speak any other languages we should be aware of?"

"We grew up close to the Spanish border. Annika and I both speak a fair bit of Spanish. I expect the men do, too."

"We have plenty of Spanish translators working this part of the world. But we'll make sure to have one on call at all times, just in case."

She went into the bathroom to push her toiletries off the counter and into her overnight bag. When she returned, Brady was fidgeting in front of the window.

He turned abruptly. "How are you holding up? Really. Be honest with me."

She stopped, considering. "I'm relieved, mostly. I was scared to death when she put her gun to my head. I hope she never does anything like that again. I guess I'm still a little shaky after that. But I'll be okay."

He studied her closely as she spoke. Was he seeing all the things she wasn't telling him? That the reasonable side of her was screaming at her to run as far and as fast as she could from this mission? That the main reason she was sticking it out was so she could be close to him? That she knew good and well she was a fool for staying in this for a man?

Her cell phone rang, startling her badly. She dug it out and frowned at the caller ID. "Pierre," she announced.

Brady nodded, abruptly all business, the moment of connection between them severed. "He's wondering where you are. Tell him you're just leaving the room and will be down in a second."

She did so while Brady zipped up her suitcase for her and set it on the floor. She disconnected the call and stuffed the phone in her pocket.

"I'll say goodbye here," he murmured. "We wouldn't want to make Pierre suspicious."

She nodded and, on impulse, stepped in front of him. "Kiss me, Brady. For luck."

He made a sound of protest under his breath, but he still stepped forward. Still wrapped her in his arms the way she loved for him to do. Still bent his head down to hers. And thankfully, this time he didn't try to lecture her about how wrong this was and how they shouldn't do it.

His lips touched hers, and the special magic between them took over. The more she kissed this man, the more she liked kissing this man. She doubted the phenomenon extended to all men, however. There was something about him—maybe the fact that he tried so hard to resist her, or that he respected her intelligence, or simply that he made her feel safe—that set him apart from other men. But she responded to him from the deepest part of her being.

He murmured against her mouth, "Everything will be fine. I promise."

"I believe you. Now kiss me some more."

He laughed quietly and ran his hands beneath her hair, cupping her head and drawing her to him. "I don't think it's legal for a woman to be as beautiful as you are."

"So arrest me," she mumbled. "Just don't stop kissing me."

"I don't think it's legal for you to be so sexy, either," he grumbled between kisses across her cheeks and jaw. He returned to her mouth as exultation burst wide open in her heart. He was willing to admit she was sexy now? My, my. The man was making progress, indeed.

Her body undulated of its own free will against his, seeking satisfaction from his and not finding it. Impatience pricked at her. Her hands roamed down his shoulders and across his chest. She wanted skin, naked and hot, against hers. She slipped her palms under his cotton shirt and groaned when his hard, muscular back came into contact with her hands.

He returned the favor, his hands roaming across her body, seeking and finding openings in her clothing and zeroing in on her soft skin. She moaned into his mouth and he inhaled the sound, breathing her desire into himself. It did something funny to her insides when he made a similar sound of frustration in the back of his throat.

"We've got no time for this," he mumbled against her lips.

"We've never got time for it," she grumbled back. "When are we going to get that?"

He pressed his forehead against hers, his eyes closed in what looked like heavy frustration. "I don't know, honey."

"Do me a favor and figure it out, okay?"

He laughed painfully and didn't answer. Disappointment ruined her mood as he took a step back. "Pierre's waiting for you."

"Right. The mission."

He sighed. "Good luck, Eve. Call me if you need anything. And if you can't make a phone call, use the phrase 'white horse' in conversation, and I'll know you need to talk."

"How will you know I said 'white horse'?"

"I'll be listening to every word you say."

The warmth that had unfolded inside her at the hotel with Brady lingered as Eve moved into the bungalow. There were no extra bedrooms—Annika had one and the three men took the other—so she was relegated to a hard, narrow army cot in the corner of the living room. She had no privacy whatsoever and had to go into the tiny, grungy bathroom and lock the door if she wanted to be alone at all. Heeding Brady's advice, though, she didn't complain about the situation.

Interestingly enough, it was Annika who first expressed hating the setup. Apparently, she was incensed that her team found watching Eve sleeping more interesting than a South American soccer game on television.

Over supper the following evening, Annika announced, "Eve, it's time to put you to work. Put on your sexiest dress and go over to the resort. You need to start establishing your cover."

The implication was clear. Eve was to pose as a hooker. Although Eve didn't think Annika had posing in mind as much as *being* one. Eve reflected behind her meek nod of agreement that Annika really was a bitch.

She rummaged through her suitcase for the naughty little sundress she'd worn the first night she'd arrived on the island with Brady. The night he'd kissed her the first time and blown her away with that sizzling embrace.

She emerged from the bathroom, and Annika scowled darkly, announcing, "That's not slutty enough."

Eve rolled her eyes. "The Three Palms is a classy place. They won't let working girls stroll around looking like cheap whores. And besides, men like their women young and girlish. Am I right, gentlemen?"

Curly grunted, "Hell, yeah. The younger the better."

André said something crude about liking them fresh, and Pierre just nodded, looking her up and down thoroughly enough to make her skin crawl.

Annika harrumphed. "Don't screw this up."

Remembering Brady's caution not to challenge the woman, Eve bit back a sarcastic comment about Annika dressing up and playing hooker if she thought she could do it better. Instead she asked, "And who am I looking for, again?"

"I told you. You'll know him when you see him." Then Annika ordered, "Saddle up, boys."

Eve frowned. "You're going with me?"

"Wouldn't want to leave our helpless little kitten all by herself, now, would we?"

Eve swore under her breath. Annika was going to make her go through with playing the slut in public. And the bitch was going to enjoy every minute of watching her abase herself for a bunch of men. It wasn't like the woman had left her any choice in the matter.

Once Eve had some poor guy alone in a hotel room, she could always change her mind and leave. It was a nasty trick to play on a man, but a girl had to do what a girl had to do. And right now, she had to keep Annika happy. Darn Brady for telling her that, anyway. He was right, of course, but it didn't sit well with Eve to let Annika exploit her like this.

They piled in the van parked out back and Curly drove

them to the Three Palms. They were one seat short, and Eve was irritated that nobody offered to let her have a seat in her skimpy dress. She sat on the ribbed metal floor in the back and did her best to keep her panties from showing as they bumped down the road.

The van stopped and Eve climbed gratefully out of the back, her legs stiff and her rear end sore.

"You can walk the rest of the way," Annika said with a note of sadistic pleasure as she noted Eve's high heels. "It's just ahead. We'll be waiting for you."

And with that, the van pulled away into the dark, leaving her alone by the side of the road under the stars. Eve just shook her head as she pulled out her cell phone and dialed Brady.

"Hi, Eve." Relief washed over her at the sound of his voice. "We'll be in place at the resort by the time you get there. The Three Palms chief of security knows who you are. He'll make sure you don't have any trouble with the staff."

"Thanks," she replied gratefully.

"You're doing great. Just keep it up," he encouraged her.

That special warmth he provoked enfolded her. She craved praise from him nearly as much as she craved his touch. "I'm off, then, to pick up some men." She added casually, "By the way, what should I charge for sex? What's the going rate for a girl like me?"

She thought she heard Brady choke briefly, but she wasn't sure. "I have no idea. Stand by. Let me get H.O.T. Watch to research that."

She kicked off her strappy stilettos and started to walk barefoot along the sandy berm toward the resort. She'd been strolling along for several minutes when Brady came back on the line. "They suggest you charge a thousand an hour or ten grand for an entire night."

Eve made a shocked sound. "A thousand *dollars?* An *hour?*

Good grief. I may have to go into the business for real. I had no idea I could pull down that much."

Brady replied dryly, "Have you not looked in a mirror in the last few years? You're an exceptionally good looking woman, Eve. Men would pay a fortune to have you."

"Thanks. I'm glad you find me so attractive." She thought maybe she heard laughter in the background at Brady's end of the call.

He answered in chagrin, "Anyone would find you attractive."

"I'm just glad you do," she replied archly. Yes, that was definitely laughter from someone standing close to Brady.

"I've got to go if I'm going to be in place by the time you get to the resort. When you get there, head for the nightclub. It's called the Monte Carlo Room."

Brady got off the phone with undue enough haste that she was still grinning when she turned into the main driveway of the resort. It turned out she had a ways to walk to reach the actual hotel, though. The grounds of this place were extensive and lushly foliaged. Plenty of privacy to be had around here. It looked like the kind of place people came to get away from prying eyes and be safely anonymous. Who on earth was Annika targeting? A celebrity? A major politician? Eve could see either type of person coming here to relax unmolested by the press or public.

Just inside a carefully casual lobby dripping in elegant island charm, a man in a well-tailored suit stepped forward to greet her. "Good evening, miss. May I help you?"

She glanced down at his name badge and was relieved to see that he was the resort's chief of security. "Hi, Leo Hawkins. My name's Eve. Could you tell me where the Monte Carlo Room is? I'm supposed to meet a friend there."

He nodded slightly as he smiled at her. "It's a pleasure to

meet you, Eve. The Monte Carlo Room is this way. If you'll come with me…"

As she followed him through the lobby, Eve glimpsed André lurking behind a pillar, looking displeased. He probably was annoyed that she was making this whole infiltrating the resort thing look so easy. Of course, it didn't hurt that she had Brady and the United States government greasing the skids for her. She smiled a little to herself.

Leo murmured as he left her at the door of the club, "Your party is waiting for you."

She jolted. Surely Leo wasn't talking about the anonymous target. Who then? Annika? She nodded her thanks and stepped inside.

It was like any one of a hundred other nightclubs she'd been in over the years. Dark, loud and crowded with insecure men and women on the prowl, desperate to make a hookup and unsure of how to go about it. In her experience, not many people were actually expert lounge lizards. Oh, sure, lots of guys thought they were suave and irresistible after a half-dozen drinks. In general, she found these sorts of places depressing.

No surprise, after getting a look at her legs in the skimpy sundress, the bouncer waived the cover fee and held the door for her. She knew not to stand in the doorway, looking around like she didn't know what to do, or the single men would move in on her en masse. Instead, she headed for the bar and immediately struck up a conversation with the bartender.

Once she'd sent out plentiful stay-away-from-me vibes she finally turned around to survey the room. The dance floor was sunken, which conveniently allowed her to look over the heads of the sweating mob of dancers and see most of the faces in the place.

"What the hell are you doing?" a female voice growled from her left elbow.

Annika. Without bothering to look at her, Eve replied, "I'm scoping out the joint for likely johns."

"You're acting like an ice bitch. Go mingle and flirt. You're supposed to be here to pick up men."

Eve turned then to look Annika directly in the eye. "I happen to have a great deal more experience at picking up men than you do. I know exactly what I'm doing. And right now, I need you to move away from me. You're killing my mojo. Talk about putting off I-hate-men vibes—everything about you screams it." The terrorist was wearing a men's tank top with wide cut armholes that barely covered her small breasts. The chain-link belt and black leather pants were typical Annika. "That whole S&M look you're going for doesn't play in a vanilla place like this."

Annika's jaw dropped.

"Shoo," Eve urged. "If you want me to find the richest guy in the joint and sleep with him, then I've got to have some room to work."

"Don't mess this up," Annika ground out.

"Only person messing anything up right now is you," she snapped. And that was when Eve spotted him. Leaning against a wall across the room, with a pair of half-drunk coeds prancing around in front of him trying to get his attention. Brady shook his head at her, a tiny movement warning her to back off and not provoke Annika.

Eve took a calming breath. "If you'll get out of here, Anni, I'll split what I make with you tonight. Please. Just let me do this my own way. I really do know what I'm doing. I practically live in places like this."

Annika slid off the tall barstool, a thoughtful gleam in her eye. Oh, Lord. Eve had just given her the bright idea of branching out into pimping female terrorist cell members. She supposed cash flow would be a major problem for someone like Annika who lived completely off the grid.

Eve picked up her drink and strolled the length of the bar. A couple of men were brave enough to toss a "Hey, baby" at her. She brushed them off, but politely enough not to put off all the men in the room, many of whom were watching her closely. As she moved slowly toward her target, she used every inch of her long legs and modeling training to full advantage. She'd likely have made it big on the fashion runways of Paris if Viktor hadn't made the entire Dupont family *persona non grata* in France.

Normally, she would skirt around the dance floor, but if Annika wanted a show, she'd give one. Still carrying her drink, Eve sashayed out onto the dance floor. Gyrating guys closed in on her like magnets to steel. She smiled and made a few moves sexy enough to whet their appetites, but not so much as to give anyone the impression she would be either easy or free.

The DJ shouted something incomprehensible into his microphone and cranked up the already blaring music even more. A few minutes out here and she was going to be completely deaf. It took her nearly the rest of the song to make her way across the dance floor, however, as the sharks closed in around her.

Of course, she knew better than to go straight for Brady. Instead, she placed herself conveniently near a large group of young people, about equally split between guys and girls. The male coeds wasted no time coming over to introduce themselves. She mentioned casually that she was in the Caymans for a photo shoot.

In under ten minutes, everyone in the nightclub would know she was some kind of cover model. And that would bring out the big money players. For some reason, men seemed to equate their annual income with the caliber of women they could reasonably expect to pick up. The college kids did, indeed, back off as a pair of men in their early thirties moved in on her.

She pegged them as finance types in town to arrange some sort of business deal. She asked just enough questions about what they did to get them going and then tuned out the steady stream of self-aggrandizing patter to follow as they tried to impress her into sleeping with them. Out of the corner of her eye, she watched Brady blow off a few more hopeful coeds. He was very good, freezing out the girls with no more than a disdainfully polite look.

A little older crowd of women moved in on him then. And these ladies were more confident and more aggressive. Eve brimmed with amusement as she watched Brady suddenly have his hands full with four cougars on the prowl.

Unfortunately, her bankers were drinking hard, and their forwardness was growing by leaps and bounds. Time to bail on these guys. She took the least obnoxious one by the arm and announced that she felt like dancing. As she passed Brady, she flashed him a brief look that dared him to join her on the dance floor.

Equal parts irritation and amusement glinted in his narrowed gaze. Didn't like watching her flirt up other men, did he? Satisfaction flashed through her. Good. She didn't particularly like watching him get pawed, either.

Her banker was an enthusiastic, if not tremendously skilled, dancer. Thankfully, he was drunk enough to want to dance with everyone around him, too, and afforded Eve plenty of opportunity to observe the comings and goings of the mob crammed on the floor.

A hand touched her elbow briefly from behind. A flare of recognition burst inside her. Brady. How had he managed to sneak up behind her without her seeing him? He was taller than most of the people here; he should have been a breeze to spot. She threw him a sidelong glance so hot it would melt most men's shoes. He smiled briefly and turned away, ostensibly dancing with a cougar who was *so* a bleach blonde and had *definitely* had some surgical work done to get that chest and that pert little nose. Her lips were suspicious, too.

Realizing belatedly that she was glaring at Brady's partner, she turned to her own partner and was mildly relieved to see that one of the coed girls from the table had come out onto the floor and was all but crawling down the guy's shirt. With a toss of her hair, Eve spun and walked away. Thank goodness that banker had made himself so easy to dump.

"Need a refill?" a deep, masculine voice said in her ear under the din of the music.

Brady. She glanced up at him and, laughing, poured the remainder of her drink on the floor. The guy whose shoe she'd just watered complained, but she ignored him. To Brady, she replied, "Why, yes. I do."

Grinning, he took her by the elbow and led her back to her original side of the club where it was marginally more quiet. He casually used his bulk to open a space at the bar for her and then tucked himself in beside her.

"Your friends are watching us," he muttered in her ear as he leaned past her to signal the busy bartender.

"Then we'll have to put on a good show," she replied. "So, sailor. Where are you from?"

He blinked, startled. "I grew up in Miami. My work forces me to travel a fair bit, though, so I'm a bit of a nomad. You?"

"French father. American mother. Living in London," she replied, keeping up the charade for Annika and her stooges.

She and Brady traded small talk for a few minutes while the bartender poured their drinks. She actually learned a few things she hadn't known about him, like his mother was his only living immediate family member, but he wasn't close to her. In fact, his jaw went noticeably tight when the subject of the woman came up at all.

The bartender passed a tab to Brady, and he casually wrote down a room number and signed it.

"You're staying here at the resort?" she asked him.

"I am. I'm here on business. Nice place. I might have to come back sometime on vacation," he answered.

She nodded. "I haven't seen the grounds. I hear they're beautiful."

"They are. Maybe when you're done with your drink you'd like a tour?"

She smiled up at him. "I'd like that." She added under her breath, "For a man who doesn't like women, you're very good at this seduction thing."

"Where did you get the idea I don't like women?" he asked a little indignantly.

She laughed. "You're kidding, right? You made it clear from the start that you have no use for them."

"Having no use for them and not liking them are two entirely different things," he retorted.

She chugged down the rest of her drink in a single gulp. "Let's take this conversation outside and continue it in private, shall we?"

His eyes blazed momentarily before he banked the fire in them. "The grounds are nearly as magnificent as you, Miss Dupont."

"Please. Call me Eve," she purred back.

"God, you're sexy," he muttered. "Is it really as effortless as it looks, or do you actually have to work at it?"

She grinned. "You have no idea how hard a girl has to work to look this cheap."

"Honey, you are a lot of things, but cheap is not one of them."

"You have no idea. I expect payment in full, in cash, in advance."

He laughed openly, then. Heads turned and disappointment

rippled outward around them as two of the most beautiful people in the joint had obviously hooked up and were out of the potential dating pool for the evening.

Brady led her out onto a patio and down a set of wide steps into a truly spectacular tropical garden. Cobblestone paths wound off enticingly in several directions.

She reached for his elbow. "I believe this is the part where I tell you I'm feeling a little tipsy and you offer to put your arm around me to steady me."

"Ah, just how I like my women," he quipped back. "Half drunk and looking for excuses to get their hands on me."

She laughed, but then broke off abruptly.

"What?" he bit out, abruptly serious.

"Is big brother listening to us?" she breathed.

"Every word."

"Oh, Lord. They're going to think I'm a complete tramp."

Brady took her hand and tucked it under his elbow as he turned and headed down a path. "I'll beat up anyone who thinks such a thing of you."

"How gallant," she sighed theatrically.

"H.O.T. Watch reports that one of Annika's boys has moved out of the hotel and is trying to follow us." He added apologetically, "I'm afraid we're going to have to take this little show to the next level."

"What does that mean?" she asked a little breathlessly as hope sprang up within her.

"This."

Chapter 11

Brady stepped forward to kiss Eve, vividly aware of how natural and easy a thing that was becoming for him. Joy unfolded in his chest at having a valid excuse to kiss her again. Nobody at H.O.T. Watch could accuse him of being unprofessional for kissing his informant to protect her cover.

Her mouth was soft and eager beneath his, the tangy remnants of her gin and tonic giving her natural sweetness a pleasing bite.

"You taste good," she murmured.

"You like single malt whiskey, then?" he replied.

"I like the taste of *you*." Her slender arms wrapped around his neck and their bodies fit together like two pieces of a puzzle. It made him think of their bodies fitted together in other ways, and his raged in response. He was getting used to being permanently uncomfortable around her and he did his best to ignore the lust bordering on pain that she aroused in him.

It didn't work, of course. The longer her mouth moved across his the more sinful his thoughts became. Except it was hard to see it as sin when Eve felt this good in his arms. He snorted. Adam probably said the same darned thing in the Garden of Eden.

He stepped back reluctantly. "That was supposed to be a getting-to-know-you kiss. We'd better cool it or your watcher might get suspicious."

"He'll think it's a free sample to entice the customer to pay for more. He won't be shocked if I let you put your tongue down my throat."

Hmm. An interesting prospect. Regretfully, he held his elbow out to her. When she took it, he continued their moonlit stroll, leading her toward the water. The sound of the ocean grew louder as they neared the resort's private beach. They stepped out of the tree cover and Eve gasped softly beside him. He smiled as she took in the pristine white sand, the bonfires at each end of the beach lending it warmth and light, and the authentic tiki hut housing a fully stocked bar.

"Like it?" he asked.

"I love it."

His cell phone rang, and it turned out to be Harry Sheffield at H.O.T. Watch, which surprised Brady. He was currently wearing an earbud with streaming live audio communications from Harry and company. Why the phone call?

"What's up?" he muttered.

"Annika's goon has followed you to the beach. He seems to be closing in and trying to signal Eve. We think he wants to talk to her. We thought you could tell her this is a business call and step away from her so Baldy can approach her."

"That's the one they call Curly," Brady replied. He put a hand over the receiver and glanced at Eve. "This is a business call. I've got to take it. Stay here and order a drink. Put it on my room tab."

She frowned, not understanding. She also knew he was wearing an earpiece. Nonetheless, she nodded and turned to the bar. He strode down the beach, out of earshot to pretend to have a private conversation. He hated to be so far away from her, but he had no choice if Curly was going to feel safe enough to move in on her.

"Let me know when he's mobile," Brady said into the phone.

"Roger." A brief pause, then, "He's closing on her."

His hand strayed to the pistol concealed in a hidden pocket at the back of his waistband. It was a compact model that didn't pack as much firepower as he liked, but it was small and easy to hide under clothes. "Call out any aggressive or suspicious move he makes."

Harry replied dryly, "We won't let him hurt your girl. The slightest hint of a threat to her and we'll let you know."

Brady winced. His girl? Was he really that transparent? And then the rest of his response hit him. He didn't mind at all the idea of her being his girl. He just didn't want H.O.T. Watch to know about it yet. *Whoa.* His mind blown, he stared unseeingly at the ocean.

Eve sipped at her mineral water over ice. The bartender had been kind enough to add a twist of lemon to it to make it look alcoholic. She wanted her head clear as long as she was working under Annika's nose.

She glanced up and started as Curly stepped out of the jungle. Speak of the devil. She pasted on a falsely pleasant expression and waited, tense, for him to belly up to the bar beside her and order a beer. The guy'd given her the creeps from the first time she met him, and further acquaintance had only heightened her unease. Annika might be violent and unpredictable, but this guy was just mean. He clearly took pleasure in causing pain, and just as clearly, he had a thing against women. Beautiful blonde women, in particular.

He mumbled in Basque beside her, which alarmed her even more than his sudden appearance. What did he have to say to her that he couldn't chance anyone around them understanding?

Initially, he groused about the outrageous cost of a beer in this joint, and then he got down to business. "Annika wants you to go back to the disco. You're supposed to be working the place."

Eve's Basque was rusty at best. She fumbled for the words to retort, "I'm *supposed* to be establishing a cover. She told me to be a hooker, and that's what I'm doing. I'm working a customer. Now go away. He'll leave if he sees me talking with you."

"You're to come back to the club with me," Curly insisted.

Irritation climbed in her gut. She switched into French to properly vent her anger at getting ordered around like this. This was a world she knew better than Annika or Curly by a mile. "Look, smart boy. Hookers at this place are not desperate junkies who charge twenty-five bucks a trick. The working girls here are high-end, and the men who hire them expect a modicum of class. Which means me not going into some club and throwing myself at every male who comes along."

Something ugly simmered in Curly's gaze, which made a shiver ripple ominously down her spine. He snarled, "I've got my orders and you've got yours. Let's go. Now." He grabbed her upper arm and commenced dragging her away from the bar.

Eve threw a panicked look down the beach to where Brady had disappeared into the shadows. No sign of him. She was on her own. In desperation, she signaled the bartender, who came over quickly. The guy'd been keeping a close eye on Curly ever since he arrived.

As Curly yanked at her arm, she resisted long enough to say to the bartender, "Will you tell my friend when he gets back that I've gone back to the Monte Carlo Room and will meet him there?"

That was all she got out before Curly hauled her away from the bar by brute force. She slogged after him through the sand, barely managing to stay on her feet as the angry terrorist stormed toward the trees. This was not good. She emphatically didn't want to be alone with Curly.

They started down a path and darkness swallowed them. The shadows and swaying palms that had been moody and romantic before with Brady were suddenly menacing. *Where are you Brady? What am I supposed to do?* Her instinct said to tear away from Curly and run like hell. But she was supposed to be bottom dog in the gang and not cause trouble. The burly man made the decision for her, though, by maintaining an iron grip on her arm that she couldn't possibly escape.

Without warning, Curly turned left, pulling her off the path and into the jungle. Uh-oh. How was Brady going to find her in this tangle of branches and undergrowth?

"Where are we going?" she demanded, her voice higher and more querulous than she would have liked. "I thought Annika wanted me at the club."

"You need an attitude adjustment first," Curly growled. "Bitchy women need to get put in their place."

Oh, my God. She was in serious trouble. How was she supposed to defend herself from whatever this gorilla had planned? Brady had warned her about this way back when. He'd tried to tell her the men she'd be working with could be brutes. Unfortunately, she hadn't even begun to comprehend him. She understood all too well now.

They emerged into a tiny clearing ringed by spiky bushes and overhung by heavy palm fronds. Brady would never find her here. Frantic, she described it for the bug in her purse. "Where is this clearing? I can't hear the beach anymore. And the palms overhead are so tall and thick. At least it's sandy underfoot."

"Shut up," Curly snapped. "Women should be seen and not heard."

"Does Annika know you think that?" Eve countered.

"She's okay. She'd put a bullet in another woman's head as fast as I would."

"Then why hasn't she done that to me, already? How come she let me live in the morgue when she had a gun to my head?"

"She thinks she owes your brother. But that sorry bastard's been dead for years. Her debt to him is expired. She's just too damned sentimental to admit it. But I'm not."

"How dare you say something like that about my brother," she hissed, genuinely furious, and also desperate to keep Curly talking until Brady could come to the rescue. *If* he came to the rescue. "At least my brother had the guts to step up and do something about his beliefs. I don't see you doing anything concrete to act upon what you believe."

He swore and called her a foul name before shoving her so hard she fell to her knees.

She popped back up to her feet fast, terrified at the idea of him getting her down on the ground and pinning her with his superior weight. What had Brady said about situations like this? Crud. They hadn't talked about situations like this. Her own street instincts took over.

She spoke with desperate calm. "Look, Curly. I talk a lot of smack, but I don't mean anything by it. It's tough to be a woman and get taken seriously. I'm just trying to get by in the world like everyone else."

"I told you to shut up." He slapped her viciously across the face before she could dodge the blow. As the sharp crack rang in her ears, her cheek exploded into fiery pain. Worse, Curly's gaze lit up with unadulterated lust. Of course. He took pleasure from causing pain. And if she was going to be a slut for some other man, why not him, too?

"How am I supposed to work the nightclub with a handprint on my face?" she demanded. "Use your brain, Curly. Annika wants me casing this resort. I can't do that if I'm too beat up to show my face."

Apparently, logic wasn't the way to this man's heart. He made an incoherent sound of rage and charged her. For a big man, he was surprisingly fast. She turned to flee, but he tackled her around the knees and knocked her to the ground, face first. Panic exploded in her brain. He was going to hurt her, and her gut screamed that he'd kill her if he could. She scrambled away from him, but he had a death grip on her ankle and inexorably dragged her back toward him.

Kicking frantically with her free leg, she caught him across the nose with her foot, and he swore violently. "You'll pay for that, you will, you stuck-up bitch. I'll show you who's in charge. I'll teach you some manners."

Eve had no desire to find out what his teaching method was going to be. No doubt it involved his fists. She stopped struggling, overpowered for the moment, but watching for her chance to escape. Something feral broke free within her. She had no illusion that this would be anything other than a fight for her life. Curly climbed to his feet, shoving her back down to her knees when she would have gotten up.

His tirade flowed around her, but she ignored it mostly, catching only fragments of it, accusations about wiggling her various body parts in front of him and teasing him, and ranting about her getting what she deserved.

He reached for her dress, and that was when it hit her that

this man was really going to rape her. The reality of it, the horror of it, hit her with the force of a freight train.

She panicked completely. Terror overrode all rational thought, and she flipped into full fight-or-flight mode. She screamed bloody murder and kicked, clawed and scratched at her attacker like a wild animal. Curly slugged her, landing a heavy fist under her jaw and snapping her head back so hard she saw stars. But she didn't stop. She kept flailing through the pain. Some part of her accepted that she was going to be damaged, maybe badly, tonight. But by God, she was going to survive. He might rape her, and he might beat her black and blue. But she would live. She went silent then, fighting grimly, forcing him to struggle for every bit of power he gained over her.

She might have put up a valiant fight, but he was bigger, meaner, and at the end of they day, a better fighter than she. Sobs of despair were beginning to break through her pants of exertion as he tore her dress partially off her and forced her down to the ground. He wedged a knee between her thighs and tried to force her legs apart. He yanked—hard—on a fistful of her hair, and the pain was so sharp her eyes watered freely.

An urge to give up washed through her. He would inevitably get exactly what he wanted from her. Why fight it? Maybe he'd quit hitting her if she just gave in and let him do whatever he wanted to her.

No, dammit. She would not let this man break her spirit. He might dominate her body, but he didn't own her. She was going to lose, but she was going to go down swinging, by golly. She fought on with renewed determination.

All of a sudden, Curly lifted away from her. It was as if a giant hand had reached down and picked up his body. Or more accurately, two hands, attached to a big, enraged Navy commander.

"Looks to me like the lady's not having fun, buddy."

She literally sobbed at the beautiful sound of Brady's voice.

"Get out of here. This is between me and the slu—" Curly broke off and then blurted, "It's none of your business. Scram." He settled into a boxer's pugnacious stance facing Brady. Eve rose to her knees and gathered the tatters of her dress across her breasts. She tried to stand up but was shocked to realize her legs wouldn't support her. She sank back down to the sand as violent trembling overtook her.

"Seeing as how the lady is with me, tonight, I believe it is my business," Brady replied coolly.

"She's a cheap whore who'll spread her legs for any man. You can have her when I'm done with her," Curly replied.

"Yes, but you're a filthy pig," Brady explained patiently. "I wouldn't take your leavings if you paid me to."

It took a moment for the depth of the insult to sink into Curly's rage-fogged brain. But then he lowered his head with a wordless howl of fury and charged like a bull. Brady side-stepped as gracefully as any matador and threw three fast, brutally efficient punches at the side and back of Curly's head as the man charged past. Brady wasn't messing around. He was fighting like he intended to take out Curly with all possible speed. And she'd seen enough violence on the mean streets of her childhood home to know she was witnessing a highly trained fighter at work. Brady delivered a vicious chop to the base of Curly's skull, and the beefy man went down heavily in the sand.

"Did you kill him?" she asked blankly.

Brady glanced down at the man in the sand and then back up at her. "Do you want me to?"

A piece of her shouted yes to that. But another, larger piece of her just wanted this nightmare to be over. She wanted to curl up in a little ball and hide somewhere dark and private for a long time. "I want to get out of here," she mumbled.

"Are you all right?" Brady asked urgently. "Did he hurt you?"

And that was when she fell apart. She stumbled to her feet and fell into Brady's arms as he swept forward to catch her. She cried hard, venting her fear and fury at being physically overpowered, releasing her humiliation at what had just happened.

He hugged her tightly through it all, saying nothing, just holding her. Curly started to come around, and Brady released her long enough to pull out some sort of short, telescoping metal rod. He rapped Curly on the back of the skull with it, and the terrorist thudded back to the ground. He didn't move again.

Brady asked her gently, "How bad did he hurt you?"

"He slapped me around and wrecked my clothes, but mostly he scared me to death."

"I got here in time to stop him from sexually assaulting you, then?" Brady asked tightly. He was crushing her so hard against him she could hardly breathe, but she didn't mind it one bit.

"You got here in time," she mumbled.

Eventually, he said quietly, "We need to get moving. Annika will get around to sending out reinforcements soon to find you and Curly and see what you're up to."

She responded bitterly, "Oh, she knows exactly what we'd be up to if you hadn't come to save me. She warned me a few days ago that Curly likes to rough up women. She knew darned good and well that he'd take the opportunity to attack me if she sent him out here alone to fetch me."

Brady went rigid against her. A frigid chill suddenly rolled off of him. Were he not holding her so close, she'd have cringed away from the icy rage of it. "We'll take her down," he said so gently it was terrifying. "You have my word of honor on that."

This was not a man to be crossed lightly. But Annika would learn that soon enough. Eve started when Brady abruptly turned her loose and moved away from her.

He spoke grimly. "You might want to turn away for a moment."

"Why?"

"I need to teach Curly a lesson and, incidentally, make sure he doesn't mess with you for some time to come."

Curious, she watched as Brady stepped into kicking range of Curly and delivered three short, hard kicks to the man's ribcage. She winced at the crunching sound of ribs breaking. Then Brady glanced up at her before delivering one more kick, harder than the others, to Curly's groin.

"That should have him living with an ice pack in his lap and absolutely no thoughts of rape for several days to come," Brady commented. "Come on. Let's get out of here."

Eve almost felt sorry for Curly. But not quite. The guy really was a pig.

Then the implications of the injuries Curly had just received sunk in. Brady expected her to continue the mission. Denial screamed in her head. She couldn't do this anymore; she didn't *want* to do it. She was scared and bruised and just wanted to go home and lick her wounds. That wasn't too much to ask, was it? Some brute had just tried to rape her and Brady had barely shown up in time. A girl was allowed to freak out and quit the job after that, right?

Brady tucked her close to his side and plunged back into the undergrowth. He led her back to a path, but if the sound of the ocean growing louder was any indication, he wasn't heading for the resort proper.

"Where are we going?" she asked.

"I have a villa. I thought you might like to pull yourself together a little bit before I take you back to the hotel."

She grimaced. She must look like hell after going a few rounds with Curly. "I didn't know this place had villas."

"The high-end guests value their privacy, and the Three Palms has special accommodations for them tucked away down by the beach. You can't believe the strings I had to pull to get one at the last minute like this."

The sound of his voice was soothing to her jangled nerves. "Talk to me about something," she mumbled. "Anything."

He seemed to understand why she asked and kept up a steady stream of conversation about the weather forecast for the next few days, when high tide would be, and commenting on the vegetation around them. He turned down a narrow path with a discreet sign announcing it to be private property with no trespassing allowed. In a few moments, a beautiful cottage came into view. It shone white in the faint moonlight, its teak shutters dark against the freshly painted stucco. The interior was equally casual-chic.

"Like it?" he asked.

"It's beautiful," she breathed.

"And you haven't even seen the best part. There's a hot tub on the veranda you can practically do laps in. Would you like to take a nice, long soak in it?"

A hot bath to steam away the feel of Curly's hands upon her skin sounded like sheer heaven. "Lead me to it."

"Why don't you go see if you can find anything in the closet to wear and I'll crank up the water jets."

Frowning, she headed for the master bedroom. The white mosquito netting artfully draped around the headboard was a perfect contrast to the rustic wood walls and log beams overhead. The palm frond ceiling fan turned lazily, and the entire space was nearly zen in its calm. She tried to let it wash over her. But it didn't sink in. She was too rattled.

And then she caught sight of herself in the full-length mirror. She looked like hell. Her hair was wild around her face, with leaves crushed into it. Her left cheek was bright red and puffy, and her right jaw was swollen enough that her face looked lopsided. Her mascara streaked down her cheeks and her red lipstick was smeared, clownlike and macabre, across her unnaturally pale skin. Her dress was destroyed, and the torn fabric barely clung to her breasts. Both knees were skinned, and her fingernails were broken and bloody. She hoped that meant she'd scratched the crap out of Curly before Brady showed up.

She went into the bathroom and washed her face. She wanted to scrub it hard, to erase the feel of Curly, but she was too tender to do more than dab it clean. She trimmed her nails and examined her knees—the scrapes were shallow and would heal quickly. She stripped naked and threw all her clothes in the trash. She'd have burned them if there were matches in the bathroom.

She pulled on a fluffy bathrobe from a hook by the shower and belted it tightly around her waist. Next, she attacked her hair, borrowing a comb from a drawer to get out the leaves and debris. She jerked and pulled at it until her eyes watered. At least that was where she decided the tears came from.

Finally, she looked in the mirror and saw nothing but herself. All traces of Curly were removed with the exception of her red and swollen face, which looked terrible. It occurred to her she had a choice: she could be embarrassed by her bruises, or she could embrace them as trophies. She hadn't given up. She'd fought valiantly, and although she'd been on the verge of defeat when Brady rescued her, she'd stayed the course. Nodding firmly at herself in the mirror, she turned out the light and went to join him. Funny, but she was sure he would see her bruises exactly the same way. He was just that kind of man.

She peeked into the closet Brady had mentioned and was startled to see a variety of casual clothes for men and women in various sizes. Apparently, the Three Palms thought of everything when it came to their guests' comfort and convenience.

She spotted exactly what she wanted and, with a smile, went into the bathroom to don it. Brady never had been able to resist her in a skimpy bikini. And for some reason, she felt compelled to reassert her identity as an attractive, sexy woman to a man she completely trusted. Her self-confidence had been shaken badly by Curly, and she needed to prove to herself she still had it.

She stepped out onto the back porch, which faced a tiny cove and white sand beach that looked as if it were lifted straight out of paradise. "Wow," she breathed.

Brady turned to face her and his gaze took her in from head to foot. A smile broke across his face. "Yeah. Wow," he replied reverently. "I swear, you get more beautiful every time I see you."

"So you like your women all puffy and bruised?"

He stepped close and barely brushed his fingertips across her jaw and cheek, but did not touch her in any other way. Panic surged in her stomach. Didn't he find her attractive anymore? Had Curly ruined her for him?

He murmured, "The moonlight has a wonderful way of making everything look flawless and fresh. You're as lovely as ever."

"You're lying, but thank you anyway."

"I'm not lying. You're perfect."

"Your delusions will wear off soon enough. Believe me, I have numerous flaws," she replied, trying to cover up how abashed she was by his compliment.

"Why don't you climb into the hot tub and tell me about these flaws of yours," he suggested. He shucked off his shirt, and she noticed he'd changed into swimming trunks. He sat on the edge of a truly enormous hot tub and swung his legs into the water.

"Be careful. I turned up the temperature earlier," he warned. "I like it hot."

"Me, too," she purred. His gaze snapped to hers, cautious and maybe a little hopeful. What was up with him? He was acting really strange. "Is your headquarters watching us?"

He shook his head. "I thought you might want a little privacy tonight. I left all the electronics inside." He glanced up at the layer of clouds obscuring the moon with only a faint glow penetrating them. "And Mother Nature has kindly provided us cover from prying eyes from above."

He slid-chest deep into the water and lounged like a gorgeous lion at rest in the tub, his muscular arms stretched out along the side of it. She felt the first stirrings of desire deep within her and nearly cried in her relief that Curly hadn't harmed that part of her. Goodness, she'd turned into a faucet tonight.

To cover her teary reaction she mumbled, "We're actually alone, then?"

"We are."

Okay, if she didn't do something to distract herself soon, she was going to blubber again, this time at how considerate he was being.

"Would you like to join me?" he asked cautiously.

Why was he treating her like she might bolt at any moment—

—Oh. He wasn't sure how she'd react to him after the earlier attack.

Uncomfortable, but knowing a moment of bald honesty was called for, she said, "Look. Curly scared the heck out of me, but he didn't rape me. I'm not irreparably scarred emotionally. Yes, I'm shook up, and yes, I'm going to be sore tomorrow. But I'll heal, and I'll get over it. You got there in time."

She stepped forward, sat down on the edge of the tub, and swung her legs over the edge, vividly aware of his eagle eyes upon her, measuring the truth of her words for himself. The steaming water was almost too hot to stand at first. Her body adjusted quickly, though, and she slid farther into the water. In a minute, she was submerged to her neck in delicious, bubbling heat.

Brady just watched her, waiting.

"Don't you believe me?" she asked.

"If you say you're okay, then you're okay. But that doesn't mean I'm about to fall on you like that bastard tried to."

She snorted. "I couldn't, in my wildest dreams, equate you with Curly. You are as different as it's possible for two human beings to be. And," she added, "you'd come out on top in every way I can think of to measure a man."

He nodded once in acknowledgement of the compliment, but a frown darkened his eyes.

"What?" she demanded.

"Now you're the one not seeing my many flaws."

She laughed. "Oh, I see your flaws, Mr. Stubborn, I don't mix business with pleasure, girls are icky."

"I don't think girls are icky!" he exclaimed.

"You could've fooled me."

He sighed. "I'll admit, my past history with women has been…less than stellar. And I may have had a tendency in the past to avoid them in general."

"A tendency?" She laughed. "You treat me like I have leprosy."

"I would never kiss a leper," he replied indignantly.

"I don't see you kissing me now," she retorted.

"And I'm not going to, either. You've had a lousy night,

and the last thing you need is to have me crawling over you like I'm no better than that—"

She moved forward through the water toward him, interrupting him. "May I?" she murmured.

He went still. The air between them went thick with anticipation. The lion was fully in command of the man at the moment. One corner of his mouth quirked up in a wry smile. "Since when do you ask?"

She closed the remaining distance between them. Gratitude flooded her that she could trust him like this. That, no matter how dangerous he was, she *knew* he'd never turn his strength or violence against her. She straddled his hips, resting her knees on the submerged bench he sat on. He held himself completely still beneath her, but tension thrummed through him. Caution and tight self-control glinted in his gaze. Darn it. He was back to being all stand-offish and refusing to respond to her.

She sighed. "Are you still trying to hold out against this thing between us?"

"Not at all. I don't know how scared you are after that ass—" He broke off, then started again. "After Curly attacked you. I don't want to scare you any further."

"I already told you. He scared me to death. But he's not you. You don't scare me at all. On the contrary, you make me feel protected and safe."

"But I'm not safe at all."

"Why not?"

His answer was slow in coming. She got the feeling that under any other circumstances but tonight's he wouldn't have answered the question at all. As it was, he sounded reluctant when he admitted, "What I'd like to do with you isn't so very different than what Curly had in mind. I'm afraid you inspire urges in me to throw you over my shoulder, haul you off to my bed and have my wicked way with you."

The idea of him doing that sent entirely gratifying desire shooting through her. Oh, no. Curly hadn't ruined her for Brady at all.

"Do you know what really scared me when Curly was coming after me? That you wouldn't get there in time to keep him from wrecking me for you. I didn't want to be so physically or emotionally broken that I couldn't enjoy you or you enjoy me." She placed her hands on either side of his face and gazed deep into his eyes. "I'm not scared of you. Frankly, being tossed over your shoulder sounds pretty good."

That preternatural stillness overcame him again. "You're sure? You're not just saying that to convince me or convince yourself?"

"What am I going to have to do to prove it to you? Throw you over *my* shoulder and haul you off to my bed to have my wicked way with you?"

He laughed. "You could try. But I'm bigger and stronger than you—"

He broke off yet again. Exasperated, she blurted, "Will you stop tiptoeing on eggshells around me? I'm fine."

He threw up his hands in surrender. "All right already. I believe you. I'll quit trying to be sensitive and caring if that makes you feel better."

Silence fell between them. What came next? Was she supposed to wait for him to make a move, or was she supposed to make the move this time because he was afraid of scaring her? She settled on saying, "For the record, thank you for rescuing me. I'll never be able to repay you."

Pain flashed through his gaze. "You don't owe me any thanks at all, let alone some sort of repayment. You put yourself at risk for me. I'm the one who can never repay you."

She moved forward, snuggling against his big body. "Hold me, please," she whispered.

His arms dropped off the edges of the tub and came around

her, his hands massaging lightly up and down her spine under the water. His fingers came up to trace her cheek lightly. "Does it hurt?"

"Not much. Tell me truly. Does it look terrible?"

"No. But even if your face was black and blue and puffed up like a marshmallow, you would still be beautiful to me."

It was her turn to gaze deep into his eyes, searching for the truth of his words. "You really don't care how I look?" she asked in disbelief.

He shook his head. "Nope."

"Seriously?" Something hopeful unfolded in her heart like the crumpled, wet wings of a newly emerging butterfly.

"Eve, you are without question the most beautiful woman I've ever had the pleasure of spending time with. But that's not what makes you special. It's your heart, your courage, your determination to do the right thing that I've fallen for."

"You've *fallen* for me?" she asked in a small voice.

He half laughed, half groaned. "Like a rock. And I can tell from that look on your face I've made a massive strategic error by admitting it."

Her heart stretched its newfound wings, eager to fly. She confessed, "If it makes you feel any better, I think you're pretty incredible, too."

His eyes blazed in the moonlight, but still he made no further advances. The man really did have amazing self-control. But she knew how to change that.

She reached behind her back and tugged at the ties of her bikini top until it came loose. "I'm feeling a little overdressed."

She pulled the scraps of cloth over her head and tossed them on the edge of the hot tub. Brady's gaze dipped to the higher curves of her breasts emerging from the bubbling water. The inferno that ignited within them warmed her all the way to her core.

"Mmm. Better," she purred. She reached under the water to tug at the ties on either side of her hips. A slight shift of her weight and the bikini bottom joined the top on the side of the tub.

"So, Mr. Hathaway. You have a naked woman in your lap and she happens to think you're the most attractive man she's ever met. What are you going to do about her?"

"I'm going to ask her if she's absolutely sure about this. I don't want her to feel pressured in any way to do anything she's not comfortable with."

"Do you always have to be so stinking responsible?" she demanded.

He laughed. "You have no idea how irresponsible I'd love to be right now."

"Show me?"

"You could tempt the angels themselves," he sighed.

"I'm only trying to tempt you. How am I doing?" She really was starting to be a little confused. Most men would be crawling all over her by now. But not Brady. No, sir. He was sitting perfectly still, waiting for…something. But what? Frustration rolled through her. His jaw rippled with clenched muscle, and that was the only answer he gave her.

In supreme frustration, she asked, "What do I have to do to get you to make love to me, Brady? Tell me. Please."

His answer was a single terse word. "Ask."

Really? That was all it would take? "Please make love to me, Brady. Take me in your arms and show me how I make you feel, and let me do the same for you. Show me what I've been missing all these years while I waited to find you."

Chapter 12

The woman was going to kill him. He'd never in his life had to reach so deep to find so much self-control as when Eve took off her bikini in his lap. Clearly the man of ice should never have climbed into a hot tub with this woman. This brave, resilient woman who truly seemed none the worse for wear after her near-rape at the hands of a brutish bastard. It had taken a fair bit of self-control not to kill Curly on the spot. Only the prospect of blowing the mission and turning a dangerous terrorist like Annika loose upon mankind had prevented him from finishing the job.

Eve had waited years to find him? Hell, he'd waited his whole life to find her. She was the exception to the rule, the one woman who'd proved to him that not all beautiful, sexy women were self-serving, untrustworthy users of men.

If anything, he was the one who'd used her. He'd taken advantage of her nobler impulses and tricked her into doing a dangerous job for him, and then he'd barely managed to save her from serious injury or worse. There was no telling if he'd get to her in time next time.

Every fiber of his being yelled at him to pull her out of the op now. To take her far, far away from Annika and her merry band of psychopaths. But it was too late to pull Eve out. Even if he did terminate the op, Annika would come after her now. Eve knew too much for the terrorist to let her walk around a free woman. His best and fastest shot at getting Eve away from Annika safely was to take down the terrorist and her cell. And that meant continuing the mission.

He shoved the unpleasant prospect away. That was a problem for tomorrow. This moment was about him and Eve. Brave, funny, outrageous Eve. Her zest for life was infectious and seduced him as much or more than her stunning beauty. He'd figured out long ago that beauty came from inside a woman, and even by that standard, Eve was extraordinary.

All of those thoughts flashed through his head in the brief interval between Eve asking him to make love to her and her arms coming around his neck as she leaned forward to kiss him. Her breasts rubbed against his chest, buoyant in the turbulent water, and he sucked in a sharp breath.

He lectured himself to go slow. She'd had a nasty shock earlier and there was no sense traumatizing her. But his hands didn't listen as they roamed across her heated skin, nor did his mouth as it roamed across her face and neck. Her hands tugged at the waistband of his swim trunks and he rose slightly to let her pull them off of him. Their bodies felt exactly right against each other and he groaned against the crook of her neck.

"Promise to tell me if you don't like something I do," he ground out.

"Okay," she panted back. "I don't like that you're taking so long getting inside me."

He laughed painfully. "I thought you'd want to take it slow and easy."

"Whatever gave you that idea?" she asked between raining kisses all over his face and shoulders. "I've been waiting to have you since that first night you kissed me on the porch. And I'm getting darned impatient, here."

"My apologies," he murmured against her mouth. Their tongues tangled together in a delicious slide of heat and wet friction that shortened his breath until he hardly recognized its sharp rasps. She tasted like lemon, tangy and fresh. Hell, she tasted like *more*. Greedily, he lapped up everything about her, the saltiness of her skin, the sweetness of her earlobes, the softness of her face, the lush heat of her mouth. Ah, the things he planned to do with that mouth....

He groaned deep in the back of his throat and she froze against him. He stopped immediately. "Everything okay?" he asked.

She smiled brilliantly at him. "I was enjoying that sound you just made. Half growl of possession, half groan of need."

"You have no idea," he muttered.

"Show me."

And show her he did. Their bodies fit together perfectly and the turbulence of the water around them did little to disguise the passion driving them together with wild abandon. It was as if she'd broken down some sort of dam within him and all the passion he'd held back for so long came rushing forth in a torrent that swept away everything in its path. Ethical considerations be damned, the mission be damned, hell, his career, his life be damned. He gave it all to Eve.

And she took all of him into herself, absorbing everything he gave her and reflecting it back, purified and somehow made sacred by the act they shared. He surged within her, half-maddened by her tightness and throbbing heat, a hundred times hotter than the water and scorching him all the way to his soul.

She cried out against his neck, and her pleasure broke over them both. He was humbled by the gift, spurred on to give her more and yet more pleasure in return. She squeezed him with her legs, pulling him deeper within her, and he surged forward until he touched her core. They found a rhythm as old as the waves breaking on shore behind them, racing forward and then retreating until he completely lost himself in the perfection of the moment. Nothing existed but Eve and the night and the two of them driving each other out of their minds with pleasure.

She cried out again, and he felt his own climax claw forward. He tried to hold it back, but he might as well have tried to hold back a tsunami. It roared forward, sweeping over him and pulling Eve with him, crashing through everything in its path and finally flinging them into a silent, peaceful place where they clung to one another, breathing hard. Just the two of them and air sliding into and out of their lungs as they panted together.

It was magical. Life changing. He ran out of words for it after that. He held Eve close in his arms, afraid she would disappear into the sea like the goddess she was. For her part, she rested her head on his shoulder, her face buried against his neck.

They stayed like that for a long time. The night grew cool around them, but the hot water protected them from its incursion. He never wanted this to end. It was the first time in his life he could remember feeling like this. He struggled to put a word to it and finally came up with one. He was *happy*.

Eventually, Eve mumbled, "I think I'm turning into a prune."

Reluctantly, he nodded. "Shall we dry off and adjourn to a proper bed to continue this cuddle?"

She rose from the water in a Venus-like fashion that Raphael would have envied and wrapped a towel she took from the stack beside the tub around herself. He followed suit, shivering as the night air hit his wet skin. He grabbed another towel and dried his hair briskly as he followed Eve into the cottage, enjoying the view of her long, tanned legs. That woman made high-fashion out of a simple towel.

She slipped between the covers as he took his rucksack of electronic surveillance equipment and chucked it into the bathroom. He closed the door firmly behind the gear. This was his and Eve's night.

Eve smiled blissfully as Brady shut the door on his headquarters' intrusion into this idyll. He was as considerate a lover as he was a boss. But she was ready for the man to be a little less considerate.

She held the covers up for him. "Come here, you."

"How're you feeling?" he asked solicitously.

"About ready for you to quit fussing over me," she replied with a smile.

"You seemed to like my fussing in the tub a little while ago."

She grinned up at him as his long body fit up against hers delightfully. "I had something a little more athletic in mind this time."

His right eyebrow sailed up questioningly.

"I want to meet the version of Brady Hathaway that would throw me over his shoulder and have his wicked way with me."

He pulled back slightly, but she followed him, pressing her body against his and savoring the sensation. She had no intention of letting him retreat from her physically or emotionally, now.

"Of course, knowing you," she said earnestly, "you're

going to take some convincing. It's lucky for you that you found a woman like me who's not afraid to show you how these things work between men and women."

A crack of laughter escaped him. "I don't need you to show me how this stuff works."

"I beg to differ," she replied in a teaching tone of voice. "You see, the woman likes the man to be strong and masterful—without being a selfish jerk, of course. We like our men to ravish us, to make us feel like we drive them a little out of their minds with pleasure. And, of course, we like the man to drive us out of our minds with pleasure, too."

He gazed down at her, amusement glowing in his eyes. "Are you finished?"

She considered him, frowning thoughtfully. "Women like orgasms. Lots of orgasms."

He was laughing again. "I believe I got that memo sometime back. Anything else?"

"Yes. Men who take too long getting around to pleasuring a woman tend to frustrate their women mightily."

"I see." He added innocently, "Is that why you've been so grouchy since I first kissed you?"

She laughed up at him and swatted his arm playfully. "Why did you hold out on me so long?"

All humor drained from him abruptly. "I was trying to do the right thing." He added grimly, "But apparently, that no longer matters to me."

She was the one who pulled back this time. "Are you saying I'm a mistake? That making love with me is wrong?"

He rolled onto his back and shoved a hand through his hair as she rose up on an elbow to wait for an answer from him.

"Hell, yes, it's a mistake. How am I supposed to send you back out in the morning to deal with dangerous morons like Curly and company? How am I supposed to casually set you up in your own room here, wondering if at any moment some bastard's going to burst in and attack you? Making love with you was a colossal mistake. But damned if I could help myself."

More hurt than Curly have ever possibly have inflicted upon her tore through her. A mistake? She was a *mistake?* An overwhelming need to flee overcame her. She rolled to her side of the bed and swung her feet out.

"Hey. Where are you going?" he asked.

"Does it matter? I'd hate to stick around and mess up your life—or, heaven forbid, your mission."

"Aw, c'mon, Eve. I didn't mean it like that. I don't regret making love with you for a minute."

The damage was done. She didn't believe him for a second. Maybe it was just her injured pride and anger talking, or maybe it was some kernel of honesty she'd been ignoring until now that made her blurt, "Did you make love to me just to get me back in the saddle, as it were? To get your precious operation back on track? Or did you actually give a damn about me for a minute, there?"

He was on his feet, throwing on jeans angrily while she yanked a sarong out of the closet and wrapped it around herself with jerky motions.

"This had nothing to do with any damned mission," he ground out. "It was only about us. I swear it, Eve."

She shook her head in sharp denial. Right now she couldn't tell if he was being honest or not. And frankly, she didn't care. The fact that he very well might be lying to her, playing her as smoothly as he had when he'd talked her into the mission in the first place, was enough to blow her trust to smithereens.

"Damn you, Brady," she said tiredly. "I'm out of here."

She all but ran from the cottage and was deeply relieved when he didn't follow her. At least he'd gotten that part right. Leave the infuriated female alone to cool off a little before continuing confrontation with said female. Blindly, she followed the path which, thankfully, took her back to the main hotel complex.

But her relief evaporated when Leo, the security guy, rolled in on her the moment she set foot in the lobby. Great. Was he going to arrest her for being a hooker now, and complete the crappiness that had been this night?

"Good evening, Miss Dupont. Your friend called and asked me to arrange a room for you. At his expense, of course. I've already taken the liberty of checking you in. Here's your key. The elevators over there will take you up—"

She snatched the key card from the man's hand and stormed over to the elevators. It was all about the damned mission, after all. God, it sucked being no more than bait in other people's traps. She was sick of everyone else using her in their own personal little games.

Shoving open the door to a posh room, fury filled her. Brady'd established her cover as a hooker, all right. She'd earned this room on her back like any proper whore.

She flung herself across the bed and burst into the tears she'd been fighting all evening. Where had it all gone so wrong? Just when she'd thought she and Brady might have it all, he had to go and mess up everything. Or had that been her who blew things between them to hell?

She finally gave in to the self-pity and cried herself to sleep.

Eve jolted awake to insistent pounding on her door. She surged out of bed, furious. If that was Brady, she was going to tell him what she thought of him in no uncertain terms. She flung open the door. "Go to he—" *Not Brady. Annika.* "—llo," she finished lamely.

Annika smirked. "Crabby this morning, are we?"

"You can go to hell, too," Eve commented sourly as she

turned away from the door, leaving it open if Annika wanted to come in.

The terrorist wanted. She stepped inside and closed the door behind her. "So what's this about a john of yours beating up Curly?"

Eve shrugged. "They got into a pissing contest about who got to have me first, and Curly came out second-best."

Annika chuckled. "He can barely stand upright, and your customer broke three of his ribs."

Eve was tempted to take Annika to task for siccing Curly on her in the first place, but reminded herself in the nick of time that the best way to get the woman's goat was not to give her what she wanted. She made a sympathetic sound. "Gee. I hope he's okay."

"He'll live. But you better hope that john leaves the Caymans before Curly catches up with him."

Eve shrugged again. "Whatever. It's no skin off my nose if Curly gets even."

"Since when did you turn into such a man-hater?"

"Imagine going through life with men hitting on you morning, noon and night. And not just any men. The crude morons who think their stupid lines will work because beautiful women can't possibly have any brains or taste in men."

The other woman nodded. "I see your point." Apparently, the sentiment put Annika in a friendly frame of mind. "I just wanted to let you know André will be taking over watching you for the next day or two."

"And what exactly will I be doing?" Eve asked.

"What you're already doing. Pick up johns. Pay for your fancy hotel room, and pass the remainder to me."

Right. As if she'd give this woman one red cent of her earnings if she was actually having to sleep with men for money. "And what will you be doing while I'm working hard?"

"Waiting."

Eve could not believe the hypocrisy of the woman. She'd send Eve out to sacrifice her body, her dignity, her soul, while Annika lounged around doing squat in the name of her cause?

Maybe it was the aftereffects of last night, or maybe she was just damned grouchy after being waken up so abruptly, but Eve snapped, "And when can we expect you to actually do something in the name of our glorious cause? Or are you all smoke and mirrors and empty words while the rest of us put our necks on the line?"

Annika sucked in a sharp breath. Her gaze went opaque. Hard. "You would dare?"

"I'm out here prostituting myself for you while you do nothing. Until I see you take concrete action to make a political statement, you better believe I'd dare." Screw Brady and his mission, and his stupid orders to play nice with Annika. She didn't feel like being nice to anyone this morning, particularly some bitchy French terrorist who thought it was good sport to sic a rapist on her.

"I'll have you know, little Miss Sunshine, that I've done plenty."

"Like what?" Eve challenged.

"You know that nightclub bombing in Jamaica a few weeks back? The one that killed thirty-three people?"

Eve nodded. Not only had Brady briefed her on it, but it had been splashed all over the news for days. Dead victims from a dozen countries had ensured global coverage for the attack.

"Yeah, well, I did that," Annika declared roughly.

Eve blinked. She hadn't actually expected a confession out of Annika. Belatedly, she remembered to look impressed. "Really? I apologize, then. I didn't know."

"Of course you didn't know. Why would I hang out a sign to every police force in the world that says, come arrest me?"

"Good point. Your secret's safe with me. Any other headlines you'd like to take credit for?"

Annika shrugged. "What's the point? What matters is the headline I have yet to make."

"How forward-thinking of you," Eve replied dryly. Thankfully, Annika seemed to miss the sarcasm behind the comment. Eve continued, "Speaking of which, I suppose I'd better get myself on down to the beach to see if this important person I'm supposed to recognize has shown up yet. And you're sure he'll show himself around the resort? He won't just head for one of the private villas and hide there the whole time he's here?"

Annika grinned wolfishly. "Oh, no. He'll show himself. He's here to meet someone and the deal won't happen unless he makes his presence known."

Oo-kay. Whatever that meant. Eve looked over at Annika. "Have you eaten breakfast? I'm about to order."

The other woman snorted. "It's nearly time for lunch."

Eve shook her head and tsked. "That's why you've got me doing this job for you. In this world, it's barely a decent hour to be awake, let alone eating."

Annika shook her head back. "The useless, beautiful people. Parasites, all of you."

Eve arched a sardonic eyebrow. "Maybe not so useless if I can spot your target for you."

"Don't get cocky. You haven't found him yet," Annika snapped.

"Have a little faith in me. I got into this resort, didn't I?"

Annika didn't bother to answer and left the room scowling. Man. And Eve thought she was grumpy in the morning!

Brady cursed under his breath and picked up the phone to H.O.T. Watch. "Did you get that? Annika just confessed to the Dred-Naught bombing."

"Roger, Commander. We got it."

He didn't give a damn if his techs were annoyed with him for making sure they did their jobs. He was in a foul mood this morning, and Annika's confession was huge. Part one of the mission had just been accomplished. If they ended the thing now, they'd still be able to arrest the Frenchwoman and put her away forever. Eve would be safe and the entire operation could go the hell away.

"Brady, are you still on the line?" It was Jennifer Blackfoot.

"What do you want, Jenn?"

"Do you have a minute to talk? In private?"

Crap. He could guess what she wanted to talk about. He had no desire whatsoever to rehash his mistakes in handling Eve, up to and including last night's fiasco. "Yeah. Sure," he replied.

"I'll be there in a sec."

Huh? The line went dead. Moments later a knock sounded on his front door. He swore under his breath. When did Jenn get into town? He opened the door reluctantly and gestured for her to come in.

"Breakfast?" he offered.

"Already ate."

"Do you mind if I eat?"

"Not at all."

He filled a plate from the spread of fruit and rolls on the buffet and carried it to the table on the back porch facing the ocean.

"Plush hideout you've got here," Jennifer commented.

He shrugged. "Someone's got to do it." And who was she to talk? She worked in a tropical paradise, herself. He surgically sliced and sectioned a grapefruit that fit his mood this morning.

Jennifer waited until he was spooning the tart citrus sections into his mouth to ask, "So did you sleep with her?"

Brady inhaled wrong and the acidic juice burned his sinuses. Coughing, he spluttered, "Jeez. Could you time your question a little more carefully next time?"

She stared at him levelly. "I timed it just fine. And you're dodging the question. I gather you did, then?"

"I don't see how that's any of your business."

"I'll take that as a definite confirmation. What were you thinking? I chose you for this mission because you wouldn't sleep with her!"

"Clearly, I wasn't thinking at all."

She swore long and freely, and he was able to finish his croissant in the time it took her to wind down. Finally, she said more calmly, "What's the damage?"

"I'd have told you the mission was blown if she hadn't just extracted that confession from Annika. Eve seems prepared to continue in spite of last night's attack by Curly and the... events to follow."

Jennifer sighed. "What did you do to piss her off so badly? Leo, the security chief, said she was all but spitting nails when he saw her last night. And she didn't sound anything like her usual self this morning."

"She decided that I seduced her to keep her from bailing out on the mission after Curly freaked her out."

"Did you?"

He shoved a hand through his hair. "How can you *think* that of me?"

"I didn't *think* you'd seduce her at all," Jennifer snapped.

"Fine. I deserve that. I suppose it doesn't help that I fought like hell to stay away from her."

"Maybe to her, but not to me."

He rubbed his temples where a headache was beginning to form. "How badly have I screwed things up?" Whether he was referring to the mission or his relationship with Eve he wasn't quite sure.

Jennifer's response left no doubt as to where she thought his mind should be. "What matters now is salvaging the mission. You and I both know we're going to come under intense pressure to arrest Annika immediately now that we've got her confession on tape."

Brady's mind raced. As much as he'd love to pull Eve out of danger and get her away from Annika and company, gut intuition warned him to see this mission through. Torn between duty and desire, he answered bleakly, "We need a little more time."

Jennifer huffed. "I know that, and you know that. But how am I supposed to convince a congressman with the parents of dead college coeds breathing down his neck that we need more time?"

"Remind them that crackpots take credit all the time for acts of terrorism they didn't commit. Tell them we're still building our case against Annika."

"That might buy us a week at most. Is that going to be enough time to wrap this thing up?"

"I don't know. But you've got to get us the extra time. We're so close. And this mission has already cost so much.…" He trailed off. He wasn't talking about money, but she knew that without him having to say it.

"Brady, Brady. What have you done? Did you go and fall in love with her?"

He lurched violently. "Hell, no!"

She studied him with her wise, dark, all-too-perceptive eyes. Dammit, what did she see when she looked at him like that? Surely not some lovestruck fool approaching middle age falling for a hot babe who made him feel young again. His relationship with Eve was a lot of things, but it was not that. She'd been as attracted to him as he was to her. And it had nothing to do with their twelve-year age gap. They'd been attracted to each other in spite of it, not because of it.

Jennifer said nothing, but her expression gradually changed to one of compassion. "You'll have to deal with that after the mission is over. What I need to know is can you do the job at hand? Can you be her handler, and will she work for you long enough to finish this thing?"

"Eve would probably be more comfortable with you acting as her handler from here on out," he admitted reluctantly. The words burned like acid on his tongue.

Jennifer nodded briskly. "All right. Once Annika clears out of the hotel and we get visual on this André fellow who's supposed to watch Eve, I'll approach her."

His gut felt like it had just fallen into a bottomless hole. It was over between them, then. He'd blown his chance with Eve. Jennifer would finish out the mission and Eve would leave, never to have anything to do with him again. How could things have gone from so perfect to so bad so damn fast?

Chapter 13

Eve was alarmed to spot Annika stretched out on a chaise lounge on the Three Palm's private beach. What was *she* doing here? Eve's nerves were still too raw from last night for her to keep up pretenses under Annika's watchful eyes today. No way was she up to playing the hooker and picking up men again. Ignoring the other woman, Eve spread her towel on a chaise lounge at the other end of the beach, lay down and closed her eyes to let the sun's warmth soothe her. Thank God the swelling was mostly down in her face this morning. Only faint redness remained from Curly's slaps. She needed this break from the mission.

Even with Annika nearby, glowering at her. Eve's thoughts kept straying to Brady. How could he have turned something so beautiful between them into a tawdry piece of manipulation? Why did everything always have to be about the job with him? If only they'd met under other circumstances, maybe they would have had a chance. Nah.

Under other circumstances he would've been working on another job and not given her the time of day.

How was it, with all the men who'd tried to win her affection over the years, that the one man she fell for wasn't capable of loving a woman? There must be something wrong with her, some flaw that prevented her from having a healthy, loving relationship with a man. Whatever it was, it sucked.

"There you are, Eve. I've been looking all over for you. I'd begun to think you were hiding from me."

Ohmigod. She cracked open one eye to glare up at Brady murderously. "Do you seriously have the nerve to face me after last night?"

He took out his cell phone and pointed it at her as if to take a picture. "Smile for the camera."

She got the message loud and clear. His headquarters was listening to this exchange. Since she didn't particularly want to air her dirty laundry to the entire U.S. armed forces, she satisfied herself with merely scowling at him as if she wished him dead.

He sat down on the empty lounge next to her and leaned in close, smiling intimately. For a moment she forgot to breathe before she remembered this was all an act.

"What do you want?" she snapped.

He spoke low under the steady background noise of the ocean. "It appears that Annika is going to be keeping an eye on you herself today. And that poses a small problem for us."

"How's that?"

"I've arranged for a colleague of mine to handle you for the rest of this mission, but we don't want Annika to see her. I can't bring her on board until your favorite terrorist clears out."

He might as well have just punched her in the gut with his fist. She choked out, "You're bailing out on me?"

He answered past a clenched jaw, "You made it crystal clear last night you didn't want to continue working with me."

"I never knew you were a coward as well as a cad."

"I was only trying to do what was best for you. What you wanted."

"What I *wanted*—"

Brady cut her off. "Smile and look like you're enjoying talking to me. Annika's looking this way."

Eve pasted on a brilliant smile and hissed, "Screw Annika."

"That's the whole point, darling."

"Don't call me that." She sounded childish even to her own ears, but it was so hard, sitting here trying to act like her heart wasn't shattering into a million pieces at the sight of him.

She would never have guessed he'd be the one to run out on her. He was actually prepared to walk out on the mission to get away from her? Wow. He must really hate her. The old feelings of abandonment flared up. First her father, then Viktor and now him.

"What's wrong with me?" she whispered.

Brady blinked rapidly. "I beg your pardon?"

"Never mind."

"There's nothing wrong with you. Nothing at all. You're pretty darned near perfect."

She pulled in a half-sobbing breath. "Right. And that's why you're beating a path to the door as fast as you can possibly get there."

"Aw, honey. I was an idiot and spoke without thinking last night. I didn't mean it the way you took it—" He broke off, swearing under his breath. "Annika's looking this way again."

Eve tensed. Why on earth would Annika be so conspicuous about watching the two of them? What was her game?

"Flirt with me," Brady ordered.

Her gaze snapped up to his. For just a moment they looked, really looked, into each other's eyes. Eve was staggered by what she saw there. Apology. Caring. And maybe even a hint of desperation. Had she misjudged him?

He wanted flirting? Fine. She'd flirt. She passed him the bottle of suntan lotion and rolled onto her stomach. He groaned quietly as he commenced rubbing the lotion into her back. Ha. Take that.

But then she was distracted by his big, warm hands kneading away the terrible tension in her muscles. Oh, my. That felt fantastic. How could she be so mad at him and yet crave the feel of him touching her? Her body was a fickle creature, curse it.

His fingers were the perfect blend of strong and gentle as he massaged her shoulders and neck. The exquisite pleasure those hands had given her last night flooded her body once more with yearning. He made a low, pained sound and she glanced back over her shoulder to see if touching her was so abhorrent to him. But what she found was a look of such desire in his eyes it bordered on wild.

Oh.

Stunned, she sat up slowly, turning to face him. "What's going on with us?"

"As much as I'd like to answer that, now's probably not the optimal time to discuss it."

She sighed. The mission. Always the mission with him. And she supposed that said it all.

He reported past a fake smile, "Annika just stood up. She's moving this way. Time for us to earn Academy Awards." And with no more warning than that, he leaned forward and kissed her. In fact, he all but gave her a tonsillectomy while he was at it. It was exactly the kind of crude kiss half-drunk men laid on her when they were trying to pick her up. Brady'd never kissed her like that before. The slap in the face it represented nearly broke her right then and there. Since when had he developed a cruel streak?

She must have made a sound that reflected the agony she felt because, as Annika's red bathing suit retreated into the trees, Brady spoke quickly. "I'm sorry about that. But, I had to make her think I want a repeat of last night with you."

Her eyes filled with tears as Brady continued frantically, "You know what I mean. A paid date. She thinks I'm a customer of yours. I was just playing a part." He shoved a frustrated hand through his hair and mumbled in chagrin, "That's not what I meant, either. Please stop looking at me like that, Eve. You know what I'm trying to say. Kissing you like that wasn't real. Surely you know how I feel about—" He broke off yet again.

She'd never seen him so flustered. Frankly, it was kind of cute. She couldn't resist poking. "I'd love to see how the guys on the other end of the radio must be reacting to that mouthful right now."

He rolled his eyes, and if she wasn't mistaken, his face was turning red. He closed his eyes briefly. He opened them and spoke once more, enunciating each word carefully. "I'm messing this up completely, and I'm sorry. I'm sorry I had to kiss you like that. I was trying to convince you-know-who that I'm still interested in hiring you. I would never kiss you like that in private because I respect you too much to treat you like that."

She studied him closely. He looked sincere. But did she dare believe him? Was she ready to give them another try? But what if he chose the mission over her again? Could she survive that?

Brady stood up. "Now that Annika has cleared out, I'm going to go get Jennifer and send her to you. She's slender, a little shorter than you, is Native American and has very long, black hair. She'll approach you in a few minutes." He paused, and then added so quietly she barely heard him, "It has been a pleasure working with you. Good luck, Eve. I wish you all the best."

He was saying goodbye? Tears filled her eyes and she squinted up at his watery image. She had no idea what to say to him. She wanted to throw herself at him and beg him not to go, to rail at him for being so hung up on the mission that he'd destroyed what they had between them. But instead she froze, cursing herself roundly as he turned and walked away.

She buried her face in her arms rather than let Brady's cameras or the resort's other guests see her cry. She'd never in her life cried for a lover before, but she did now. She cried silently for her loss and loneliness, for what could have been and for what never would be. She highly doubted she would ever find another man like Brady, and she cried at having blown her best, and likely only, chance at love.

Eventually, she cried herself out. She made a halfhearted effort to pull herself together before this Jennifer person showed up. Sniffing, Eve toweled off her face. Her eyes were probably red and puffy and there wasn't much she could do about that. But she could at least compose herself. She rolled onto her back and sat up, surveying the beach from behind a pair of sunglasses. Tall, slender, long, black hair. Her new handler shouldn't be too hard to spot.

She scanned the people on the beach, looking for this Jennifer. In fact, a woman had just stepped out onto the sand at the far end of the cove, when another face caught Eve's attention. It was a man, just leaving the beach. She didn't see him for long before he disappeared into the trees. But it was enough. She *knew* that face.

"Holy Mary, mother of God," she breathed. Shock poured through her like ice water, freezing her into immobility.

Her phone rang immediately.

She fumbled for it in her bag and finally put it to her ear. It was Brady. He sounded like every molecule of the soldier within him was on full battle alert. He knew her too well. "Talk to me, Eve. What do you see?"

"It can't be. He's dead."

"*Who's* dead?"

"I know who Annika's here to kill," she announced.

"Who?"

"Her brother. I just saw Drago Cantori."

"Where is he now?"

"He left the beach and headed down one of the paths toward the villas."

The dark-haired woman at the far end of the beach swerved into the trees abruptly. Yup. That had been her new handler, no doubt called back to the hotel for an emergency briefing with Brady and whoever else was here on behalf of Uncle Sam.

"Does Annika know he's here?"

"She left the beach a while ago. If she didn't spot him arriving at the resort, I'd say odds are she doesn't know he's here, yet."

"How will she react to seeing him again?"

"I have no idea. She and Drago had a strange relationship. Intense. A love-hate thing. I think their father forced the two of them to compete against each other a lot. They had their hatred of him in common, but they were forever being pitted against one another. Does that make any sense?"

"It makes perfect sense. Don't question your instincts, Eve. They're solid." He paused, then asked, "Would Drago recognize you if he saw you?"

"Absolutely."

"Why are you so sure? You would still have been a young girl the last time he saw you."

She answered reluctantly, "The last time he saw me, he

tried to rape me. I was about a foot taller than him and beat him up. I can't believe he would forget that, or my face."

Grim silence met that revelation. Finally, Brady bit out, "I'm so sorry I got you into this, Eve."

"I volunteered, remember?"

"After I manipulated you into it."

"Nobody forced me to come here. Get over your guilt trip and do your job, already."

That earned her another long silence. Then, "Look, Eve. This may change things. I'll do my best to stay out of your way, but I may need to stay on this mission."

It was pathetic how her heart leaped in her chest. She tried to answer evenly but had no idea if she succeeded or not. "I'm okay with that."

"Jennifer's here. I've got to go. Stand by for further instructions."

"Roger, Batman," she said with mock severity.

She caught his reluctant chuckle as the line disconnected. Son of a gun. Drago Cantori. Memories of the mean child and vicious teen he'd been flowed through her, making her shudder. If there was a bigger monster loose in the world than Annika, surely it was her brother. Eve might have come out of their past encounter relatively unscathed, but after that brief glance of the big, beefy adult he'd become, she doubted she would fare so well against him if there was a repeat encounter.

Her cell phone rang again, startling her. It was Brady's number. "Yes?"

"Can you come to my villa?"

"When?"

"Now."

Butterflies took flight in her stomach. "I'll be right there."

Brady couldn't believe he was actually nervous to see Eve. Maybe it was seeing her here in his villa, in the place where they'd made love and everything had changed for him, that made him so agitated.

"Are you all right?" Jennifer asked.

Damn, that woman was too perceptive for her own good. Of course, it was what made her the outstanding CIA field agent that she was. He sighed. "No. But I'll live."

A quiet knock sounded on the door and he tensed. He opened it, and as always the sheer flesh impact of Eve's beauty stopped him cold for an instant. "Hi. Thanks for coming."

"It is my job, is it not?"

Right. The job. Strange that she'd be the one to invoke that. She'd been busy trying to convince him to ignore the mission in favor of their personal relationship almost from day one.

She stepped inside. It pained him to see how she moved to the opposite side of the room from him and avoided making eye contact with him. Yep, he'd blown it big when he'd invoked the mission last night immediately after making love with her. He should've told her how he felt about her. Told her how she'd rocked his world and changed his opinion of women, how she'd earned his trust and respect—dammit, how much he cared for her and wanted to give whatever was growing between them a chance to develop and mature.

But instead, he'd frozen up like some raw recruit and fallen back on his soldier persona in panic as soon as the subject of feelings came up. He had a sinking certainty in his gut that he was going to regret that incident for a very long time to come.

Jennifer was speaking. "—recognize you?"

"Yes, I'm positive. I haven't changed in physical appearance much from when we were fourteen, and Drago's no dummy."

Jennifer sighed and glanced over at him. He swore under

his breath. Punting the unpleasant question to him to ask, was she? He glared at his CIA counterpart briefly before turning reluctantly to Eve. "I'm duty bound to ask you, Eve. Would you be willing to make contact with Drago?"

As he expected, her eyes went wide with alarm, and she folded her arms tightly around her middle. "Why?" she asked in a strangled voice.

"Annika's likely to ask it of you. If you refuse, she may get suspicious, or worse, start to see you as a liability. She may try to take you out."

"You mean she'd try to kill me?"

He winced, but he owed Eve total honesty at this juncture. "That's correct."

She sat down on the sofa and all but curled into a little ball in the corner of it. His arms ached to hold her and comfort her, but there wasn't a damned thing he could do about the situation.

"What would you want me to say to him?" Eve asked in a small voice.

Brady sat down cautiously on the far end of the couch and gazed at her candidly. "You're not going to like the next part of this. Our profilers think the best way to approach Drago will be to pose as a call girl and offer him sex."

Eve reared back hard. "It's one thing to flirt with you. But Drago?"

He continued quickly before she could refuse out of hand. "We wouldn't expect you to actually go through with it. Rather, we'd want you to string him along. Keep him waiting for you to, uh, deliver. It would serve as a powerful distraction tactic, throw him off balance while we figure what he's doing here."

"What *is* he doing here?" Eve demanded.

"We don't know. Our surveillance shows that Annika hasn't made contact with him. In fact, we believe she actively avoided seeing him or being seen by him. We've reviewed our surveillance footage, and she received a cell phone call moments before she left the beach, and only a few minutes before he arrived on the beach. We think one of her men may have called her to warn her that he was coming."

Eve frowned. "If her other guys were watching for Drago and spotted him first, why did she want me here at the resort to look for him?"

"Are you sure her brother is the target of her planned assassination?" he asked.

"I'm sure. She was adamant that I would recognize the target the moment I saw him. It seemed to amuse her, in fact."

Jennifer interjected, "Does Annika know about Drago's attempted assault on you?"

"Oh, yeah. She teased him mercilessly about how I beat him up in front of the other kids at school. He left school for good just a few weeks afterward. I always wondered if the humiliation was too much for him to stand."

It made sense. And it also meant that Drago would have a massive chip on his shoulder where Eve was concerned. He might very well want much more than sex from her. He could want revenge.

Brady swore mentally. He'd barely managed to save Eve from Curly. What if he didn't get to her in time the next time? The thought of Eve seriously injured or worse at some thug's hands was too much for Brady. He jumped to his feet. "We can't do this. It's too dangerous. Eve could get hurt."

Jennifer frowned at him. "We agreed we would let her make the choice. If she wants to approach Drago, we'll take all possible precautions, but we'll let her do it."

Brady shook his head in denial. He opened his mouth to protest, but Eve cut him off.

"Oh, now you're suddenly all concerned about me? You warned me over and over that this would be dangerous and that I might die, but it didn't stop you from recruiting me. You also said I could prove once and for all that I'm not a terrorist. I happen to be willing to risk my life to do that. It's not your call to make, Brady."

"You have no idea what you're getting into!"

"Just like I had no idea what might happen if I let Curly drag me into the jungle? Haven't you asked yourself why I didn't make a fuss when he took my arm and forced me to go with him? Why I didn't call down the beach to you for help? I was willing to risk him attacking me to maintain my cover. The *mission*—" she spat the word out "—is that important to me. Can you say the same?"

"This isn't a pissing contest to see who can take the most risk. This is your life we're talking about."

"I know that."

He seriously doubted she did. She was just mad at him and out to prove that she could be as stubborn and pigheaded as him about pursuing Annika at all costs. "I can't in good conscience take advantage of your anger at me and allow you to do this."

Eve threw up her hands. "Oh, get over yourself, Brady. Not everything is about you."

That stopped him cold. Was he really that self-centered? He prided himself on being levelheaded at all times, particularly when a mission was on the line. He was rational. Self-disciplined. He glanced over at Jennifer for support and was stunned to see her smirking at him. She agreed with Eve?

He hated everything about letting Eve make contact with Drago in the guise of a high-priced call girl. Something hot and ugly chewed at his gut, and he was shocked to realize it was jealousy. At some level, he considered Eve to be his woman. And he didn't like the idea of her throwing herself at another man. Even if it was a ruse. He sat down heavily.

Jennifer took over briefing Eve and he listened, numb. "We

expect Annika will want you to make contact with Drago, possibly to set him up for the kill. She may try to suggest you get him in bed, maybe drunk or drugged. Then, when he passes out, she'll move in for the kill."

Brady didn't miss the shudder that passed through Eve, but he also didn't miss the defiant look she threw him immediately. He cursed steadily in his head. This was bad, bad, bad. Every fiber of his being shouted it at him.

Jennifer continued, "We'd suggest you insist on a kill in a more public location. Tell Annika it won't look like a political statement if he dies in bed with a prostitute. It'll look like a jealous girlfriend offed him. If Annika wants to send a message, he needs to die out in the open. Convince her to have you set him up someplace else. Maybe on the beach, or at the outdoor restaurant by the hotel."

Eve frowned, thinking hard. "Could I say something about it being easier for her and her guys to get away after the kill?"

Jennifer smiled brightly. "That's an excellent idea."

No. It wasn't. It was a terrible idea. It would encourage Annika to put Eve only a few feet away from Drago when someone who was not a trained sniper took a long-range shot at Drago. If the idiot missed, Eve would be hit. Hell, if Curly took the shot, he might hit her intentionally.

His thoughts jerked back to the present when Eve asked, "Why do you suppose Annika wants to kill Drago?"

Ah. The sixty-four-thousand-dollar question. He watched grimly as Jennifer replied, "We have no idea. We were hoping you could find that out for us. Maybe ask Annika that very thing?"

"I don't know if she'd tell me," Eve replied. "I don't think she entirely trusts me."

He burst out, "That's all the more reason not to throw you into the middle of a potentially explosive situation!"

"That ship has sailed," Eve replied without emotion. "I'm doing this, and that's that."

Then she was going to die. And there wasn't a damned thing he could do about it.

Chapter 14

"Annika, you'll never believe who I just saw," Eve announced excitedly.

The terrorist had knocked on Eve's door not more than two minutes after Eve got back from Brady's villa. She hoped the Frenchwoman hadn't been waiting for her and the timing was just luck, but she couldn't be sure.

"Let me guess. You saw a ghost."

Eve stared. "You knew Drago's alive?"

"I suspected."

"What's he doing here?" Eve asked.

Annika's cold smile sent shivers down her spine. "He believes he's here to make the deal of a lifetime."

"I don't understand."

"It seems that brother dearest has become a bit of a merchant since his supposed demise."

"A merchant? What kind of merchant?"

Annika paced in agitation. "He sold out. He's become

an arms dealer. Worse, he does business with governments. Oppressive regimes that squash the rights of the common man. That use his weapons to kill innocent women and children. That ally themselves with the very governments we've spent our lives trying to topple."

"You said he believes he's here to make a deal? Is it a ruse?"

Annika laughed in delight, but the bloodthirsty echo of it was chilling. "Oh, no. The deal is real. But instead of getting rich, he's going to die."

"For real this time?"

"Exactly. And you're going to help. You won't mind seeing Drago dead, will you, beautiful Eve? You haven't forgotten what he tried to do to you, have you?"

Eve let the revulsion at the memory show on her face. "I haven't forgotten. What can I do?"

"I need you to set him up. If he sees me, he'll know something's up. But you…he'll never suspect you. Or if he does, he won't care. His desire for revenge will blind him. He always did think you were dumber than dirt. His mistake, huh?"

Eve shrugged. At least Annika didn't think she was completely stupid. Just stupid enough to be bait to lure Drago. "I'm in."

"Put on your nastiest dress. Do your hair and makeup and flash those legs and breasts of yours at him. Get him drunk. You can slip him a roofie if you like. Take him to bed. And when he's snoring on your breast, that's when I'll kill him."

The avid enjoyment in Annika's voice as she anticipated killing her only living relative was sickening. Not to mention Eve was getting really tired of Annika's fixation with getting her to look and act like a slut. Jealous much, was she?

Remembering the briefing with Jennifer and Brady, Eve shook her head. "If you kill him in bed with a woman, his death will lose all impact. People will think a jealous lover killed him. If you want to really wreck his reputation you need to kill him in public."

Annika cut her off. "No! No one can know he's dead."

Eve blinked. "I beg your pardon?"

"Don't you see? I'm going to become him."

"But," she frowned, "I thought you said he'd sold out."

"He did. But he has created a lucrative business and impressive contacts. I can take it over. Turn his resources away from corrupt regimes and feed them to true freedom fighters."

"But you're not him. How do you know his suppliers will do business with you?"

Annika snorted. "Haven't you heard that blood is thicker than water? You, of all people, should know. If there's one terrorist in the family, you can count on the whole family being terrorists, eh?"

Eve stared, stricken. Was Annika right? Was she doomed always to carry the specter of Viktor's politics around with her? Would she never shake the taint of being a Dupont? She mumbled some sort of agreement with the other woman.

Annika continued, "We'll do it tonight. Drago has a private villa. He'll no doubt have security guards with him. Make them leave the room when you…" Annika made a crude suggestion for what Eve should do with her brother to distract him.

Not in a million years would Eve let Drago do such things to her. She'd kill herself first. But she bit the inside of her cheek and didn't interrupt Annika. Brady must be having a fit right about now. It served him right.

Annika was still speaking. "…take the shot. Then you will help the boys carry his body to the ocean. I'll have a boat waiting and we'll drive him out to sea and dump him for the sharks."

"What about his guards?" Eve asked.

Annika shrugged. "Drago knows better than to trust anyone close to him who carries a gun. He won't depend on them to protect him out of loyalty. They'll be mercenaries and well paid. They'll work for the highest bidder, no questions asked. After he's dead, I'll offer them continued employment working for me. They know the score. They'll take the job or I'll kill them. And in the meantime, I'll pay them better than he did."

"You seem to have thought of everything," Eve commented.

"My sources say Drago will meet his buyer in the restaurant at the main hotel. I'll see to it the buyer doesn't show up tonight. Your job is to wait until it's clear that Drago has been stood up, then move in on him and work your stuff. Are you clear on what you're to do?"

Eve nodded. Annika seemed to expect her to say something, so she murmured, "How hard can it be to pick up a man? Especially one who's tried to bed me before? Piece of cake."

Except her stomach was churning, and she suspected it was only going to get worse before this night was over.

Not long after Annika left her room, Jennifer knocked on Eve's door. Eve wasn't sure if she was glad for the company or not. A tiny part of her wished it was Brady briefing her on the last details of tonight's operation.

"Okay, Eve. You're to do as Annika instructed. Meet Drago in the restaurant and go back to his villa with him. When Annika and her men move in to take the kill, we'll jump them and take them down. They should never get close to you."

"Yeah, but Drago will."

"We'll send in a second team to stop him before he can get frisky with you."

"What if he pulls a Curly and decides to just drag me into the jungle?"

"Then we'll take him down right there and pull you out. Annika and her men should already be in place at the villa for the kill by then, and we can still spring our trap on them. Remember, we've got state-of-the-art surveillance equipment, a team of highly trained operatives and the best technical support in the business for this operation. You'll be perfectly safe."

Eve noted wryly that Jennifer didn't make any promise to that effect, however. "Will I have bugs on me?"

"We can use the one in your purse, but we can't risk putting one on your person. As much as I'd love to give you an earbud so we can talk directly to you, Drago would flip out if he found it. And if he's anything like Annika, he's cautious enough to look for such things."

Eve snorted. "He's like Annika, all right. But worse. She's the calm, rational one of the two of them."

Jennifer made a face. "I wish I had enough evidence to take him out while we're here. But unfortunately, he's not the focus of this investigation, and I have no hard evidence to incriminate him in any crime. This is the first we've heard of him being alive, let alone him being an arms dealer."

"If he gets away, you'll go after him, though?" Eve asked warily.

"Count on it," Jennifer replied grimly. Into the ensuing silence, the other woman asked, "So. Have you decided what you're going to wear?"

"I picked up a little outfit in the resort's boutique a while ago," Eve answered. "I charged it to my room, so you're paying for it. I hope you like it."

"As long as it catches Drago's eye, everyone will be thrilled."

Except for Brady. Truth be told, Eve had picked the dress

specifically for its capacity to raise his blood pressure and infuriate him.

"There's one more thing," Jennifer said soberly.

Eve looked up sharply. What had put that serious tone in her new handler's voice?

"Brady insisted on it. He threatened to blow the operation if I didn't agree to it. Threw quite a tantrum." Jennifer reached into her handbag and pulled out something black, leather and triangular.

Eve frowned as the other woman laid it on the coffee table in front of her.

"It's a gun. Brady insisted you have it to protect yourself if things don't go well tonight."

Eve stared in shock at the compact weapon in its holster. What did it mean? Was he trying to send her some kind of message?

"That's a thigh holster. I figure Drago's men may search your bag, but they won't likely frisk you. Drago will want to do that himself. It has a quick, silent release here—" Jennifer demonstrated how it worked "—so you can take it off fast and hide the gun if it looks like Drago's about to find the weapon."

Eve picked up the weapon and holster and examined them cautiously.

"Please tell me you've shot a pistol before," Jennifer remarked.

"Brady taught me how to shoot," she replied absently, still occupied with figuring out why he felt compelled to arm her before her encounter with Drago.

"You might want to review what he taught you now. And practice pulling the gun a few times once you're dressed. A bit of dexterity is required to flip up your skirt and grab for the gun all in one move."

And with that piece of advice, Jennifer excused herself, claiming to have other preparations to see to.

Eve had plenty of her own preparations to do. She painted her fingers and toes with brilliant red nail polish, She curled her hair into a flowing mane, and she took special care with her makeup. They wanted her to play a femme fatale and that's what she'd do. The more makeup she put on, the more striking she became. She shook her head at the mirror. Even made up like a raccoon with black rings of makeup coating her eyes, she looked more exotic than ever. Cursing her beauty, she moved on to the dress.

It was a sleeveless mini, made of wide straps of flesh-colored girdle material sewn together on varying diagonals. It hugged her body tightly, leaving very little to the imagination and making her look buck naked at a glance. She wore no jewelry to distract from her face or her body.

She had to turn the pistol holster so the gun rested on the inside of her thigh, but thankfully, the hem was long enough to cover the black leather. She supposed if a bit of it showed, people would just put the leather garter down to being some sort of fashion statement.

She slipped on impossibly high-heeled shoes and slipped her MP3 bug, her phone and her room key into a crystal-encrusted clutch. She was ready to go. Now all she had to do was wait for the call. One way or another, the mission would end tonight.

And Brady Hathaway would be out of her life for good.

Coordinating an operation on this scale was a nightmare, but even the demands of multiple teams of operatives with a variety of tasks wasn't enough to distract Brady from the low-level hum of panic in his gut. As sure as he was standing here, something would go wrong tonight. And Eve would get caught in the thick of it.

His villa looked more like a miniature version of H.O.T. Watch headquarters than a cottage. A bank of video monitors took up one side of the living room, a team of special operations controllers seated before them. Weapons and communications equipment took up most of the other side of the room, and a pair of Caymans police officers took up the remaining space, ready to coordinate with their headquarters should additional support be required.

Everything was in readiness. He'd personally checked and rechecked all the equipment. But of all people, he knew that no matter how thoroughly they planned an operation, something would always go not according to plan. And that unknown was what scared the hell out of him.

"Drago's on the move," someone announced.

His gut clenched so hard it cramped. Brady gripped the back of the controller's chair and watched Annika's brother stroll with a pair of bodyguards toward the main hotel. They were hoping to spot whoever Annika was going to waylay this evening, to get an idea of who Drago was selling illegal weapons to. It would be a nice side benefit of this mission if they bagged a major weapons dealer and his customer, too.

"Any movement from Annika?" Brady asked.

"Negative. She's still in a car hidden by the side of the road. Looks like she's still planning on causing an accident."

The decision had been made to let her succeed at stopping the buyer and to let her rendezvous with her men outside Drago's villa. Annika's men were scattered across the resort at the moment, and catching them individually without tipping off Annika and causing her to flee could be difficult, if not impossible. Better to let them all come together before H.O.T. Watch sprang its trap.

In quick succession, Jennifer, seated at a table in the restaurant, reported that Drago had entered the room, and the satellite surveillance tech watching Annika reported a limousine approaching the hotel. The expected car accident happened, and all eyes were glued to the monitors as the vehicles crunched together.

The limousine didn't stick around for its occupants to get out and examine the damage, however. Brady and company watched in chagrin as the big, black car turned around on run-flat tires and its powerful engine roared. The limousine raced back toward George Town, and presumably the airport.

A brief flurry of activity ensued as the Caymans police were asked to dispatch a team to intercept the limousine.

But then, the order Brady'd been dreading all day came across his headset. Jennifer muttered, "Drago's getting jumpy. Send in Eve."

Brady gritted his teeth and dialed a number on his cell phone.

"Yes?" Eve sounded nervous. Smart girl.

"Are you sure you want to do this?" he asked without preamble. "It's not too late to back out."

"Don't make this harder than it has to be."

"All right," he replied quietly. "You're up to bat. And promise me you'll be careful."

All she said was, "I'll do the right thing." And then she hung up.

He swore violently enough that a couple of the controllers looked over their shoulders at him in concern. "Eve's on the move," he reported tersely.

He leaned over the shoulder of the man tasked to watch Eve. The tech was using a feed to the hotel's discreet, but numerous, security cameras. Eve stepped out into the hallway and Brady sucked in his breath hard.

"Is she wearing any clothes?" the controller asked in minor shock.

Brady had to look again to see the barely there dress clinging to every familiar, fantastic curve. His body responded so hard and fast it nearly brought him to his knees. What in the hell was he doing? He couldn't let her go through with this! The mission be damned. His career be damned.

"Harry," he bit out, "you're in charge." He spun and headed for the door.

"Where are you going?" the controller called after him.

"Keep me informed at all times of Eve's movements." And with that he slipped out into the night. For the first time since Eve had stormed out of the villa the night before, he felt like he was doing the right thing.

It was a short walk from the elevator to the restaurant, but it was plenty long enough for her to question the wisdom of wearing this dress. To say it stopped traffic was an understatement. It appeared to be turning every adult male who saw her into a drooling statue.

She stepped into the restaurant and waited patiently while the maître d' stammered through asking her where she'd like to sit. He supposedly had orders to parade her past Drago's table, and he eventually collected himself enough to mumble, "This way, mademoiselle."

She followed him into the open space and felt the weight of every stare in the room upon her. She spotted Jennifer sitting over by the window with a man Eve didn't recognize, and even the two of them were staring at her. Obviously, she was good at playing the part of a siren.

Eve couldn't bring herself to make eye contact with Drago immediately. She waited until she was nearly at his table to look up. Sure enough, he was staring a hole through her. He was about twice the size he'd been in every dimension since she'd last seen him as a scrawny teen. His neck bulged like a bulldog's, and his shirt strained across muscles any bouncer would envy. His eyes were small, black and as truculent as ever.

"Drago?" she asked tentatively. "Oh, my God! Is that you?" It was all she could do to act pleased to see him when her insides were quailing at the way he was already stripping her dress off with his eyes.

"Eve Dupont? What the hell are you doing here?" His voice was the gravelly growl of a heavy smoker.

Uh-oh. He sounded suspicious. Not good. Did he smell a trap?

She slid into the seat across from him without waiting for him to ask. His two bodyguards—men every bit as burly as their boss—bristled belatedly, but they seemed as bemused by her nearly naked state as everyone else.

"I'm on vacation," she gushed. "I live in London now. I can't believe you're… I heard you were… When Viktor died… I'm so glad you're alive!"

Drago continued to look far too suspicious of her. He leaned back in his chair to study her. "Have you heard from my sister since Viktor passed?"

She made a little face and leaned forward to confess, "I have to admit I never liked Annika much. And I don't think she had much use for me, either. I never did understand what Viktor saw in her."

Drago laughed, an ugly sound that only tightened the knots in her gut. But at least the wariness in his expression eased fractionally. "So. What are you up to these days, little Evie?"

She shrugged. "I do some modeling. Between jobs I party a bit."

His eyes lit with the same unholy madness that all the Cantoris' eyes did. He hadn't missed her oblique reference to being a call girl. That might have been the goal, but she suddenly had to go to the bathroom very badly. She pressed her knees together tightly. The pistol high inside her thigh bit into her leg comfortingly. And all of a sudden, she knew exactly why Brady had given her the gun. He wanted her to know he was with her, looking out for her. Keeping her safe. A wash of gratitude rolled through her.

"Who are your friends?" she asked coyly, and hopefully flirtatiously.

"Luger and Hans. They work for me." Drago explained to his companions, "Eve here is from my hometown. She and I went to school together. You might say we have a history between us. Unfinished business."

Her gaze faltered. He hadn't forgotten. Or forgiven. Oh, God. Oh, God.

He was speaking again. "…looks like the bastard's stood me up. What say we party tonight, you and me? For old times' sake. We can finish that business between us."

Her courage failed her and the words tumbled out of her mouth before she could stop them. "I don't think so—" She broke off in horror as she realized what she'd done. She backtracked hastily. "I don't think you could afford me, Drago."

He laughed heartily. "I'm a prosperous businessman these days, little Evie. Even though I believe you owe me…" he let the threat hang in the air between them for a moment before continuing "…I'll pay you double your usual rate. Triple. But in return, you do whatever I say. Anything I want."

Gulping, she tried hard not to picture what this animal would demand of her. She was supposed to be a call girl. A professional. She had to act like one convincingly.

"Drago, I remember you very well. And I can't afford to be out of action for long. It's going to take me a while to… recover from you, am I right?"

His gaze burned wildly. "You like it rough, do you? I woke something kinky in you, did I?"

"Something like that," she murmured reluctantly. "My going rate is ten thousand dollars U.S. a night. I figure at least a week to heal…plus pain and suffering. Say, a hundred thousand?"

He leaned back hard. "No whore is worth that much."

"Ah, but how much is satisfaction worth? Revenge? Putting the whore in her proper place?"

She didn't know what it said about her that she knew exactly what buttons of his to push. But a fine sheen of sweat broke out on his forehead. "I have one condition, though," she added silkily.

"What's that?" He was panting so hard with lust he could hardly talk.

"You have to promise not to cause me any permanent damage."

"But anything else goes?" he growled.

"For a hundred grand, anything goes." She swallowed the bile that rose into her throat as he nodded and gestured sharply to a waiter.

"Put the food on my bill," he snapped at the man. The waiter barely got a chance to reply before Drago was on his feet beside her, taking her by the arm and hauling her to her feet. His fingers dug into her skin painfully, a foretaste of things to come if he had his way.

Drago leaned close to whisper in her ear, "I've been waiting a long time for this. A very long time, you little bitch."

Her legs nearly collapsed out from under her. It was all she could do not to bolt for the far side of the room and Jennifer. She could do this. She had to do this. To clear her name. To prove to Brady that she was strong and brave and didn't need him. To prove to herself that she didn't need him.

What in the hell had she gotten herself into?

As Brady listened in horror to the live audio feed directly from Eve's bug, he broke into a run. That bastard was planning to torture Eve, maybe even kill her. Either way, she was in serious, serious trouble. He veered away from the main hotel and headed toward the far end of the resort where Drago's villa was located.

"How much of a head start do Drago and Eve have on me?" he panted.

"Unknown," Harry Sheffield bit out. "I've got cloud cover at the moment. It should pass within three to four minutes."

Three minutes? Eve could be dead by then. Cursing, Brady lengthened his stride.

"Dude, you can't just bust down the front door of the villa," Harry said urgently. "We've got a hunter-killer team about to barge in there guns blazing. You can't blow their positions. You know better." He added desperately, "Eve will die if you don't get your head together."

Dammit, Harry was right. "Talk to me. Where are our people deployed?"

"They're positioned exactly as briefed."

He thought fast about the layout of the villa. The master bedroom faced the ocean. "Tell them I'm approaching from the beach side of the cottage."

"Sir, there's no cover from that side."

"Then I'll have to be especially sneaky, won't I?" he snapped.

"Sir—"

"You can either help me or just hope I don't screw up your op."

Harry sighed. "You're going to end your career over this."

Brady said something rude enough back that Harry laughed reluctantly.

"All right, Commander, here's the deal. As long as there's cloud cover, you should be able to move up the beach if you're careful. But once the moon comes back out, you'd better be under cover. It'll be as bright as day out there."

"Roger," Brady replied.

He ducked off the path and headed for the beach. He ran in the heavy sand, oblivious to the effort it required. Eve was in trouble. He would run barefoot through broken glass to save her.

He reached the first private beach and crossed it fast. He had to wade through knee-high water around the artificial barrier of rocks and vegetation to reach the next private beach. He crossed this one as well, then slowed to ease around the next barrier and onto Drago's private beach.

Harry murmured, "The hunter-killer team reports that Drago and Eve are arriving at the villa now."

Brady clicked his microphone switch once by way of reply. He moved forward through the shadows at the edge of the beach. Lights came on inside the structure. And in moments, the bedroom light switched on. Eve entered the room first as Drago shoved her hard, throwing her down across the bed. The terror on Eve's face was more than Brady could stand. He reached for his weapon, a short-muzzled MP-7 assault rifle and swung it up into a firing position.

But then one of the guards stepped into the doorway. Brady swore under his breath and lowered his weapon. If he killed Drago with that guy around, the bodyguard would shoot back. And if the guy was any good at all, he'd start by killing Eve before progressing to whoever was beyond the window.

Drago backhanded Eve across the face, and Brady flinched as hard as Eve did.

Harry announced, "Team two reports that the Three Stooges are in sight. We're still awaiting Annika's arrival, but she should be on the property by now."

Brady eased a little closer to the villa, giving himself a better angle to cover more of the bedroom with his weapon. But it also put him farther out on the beach.

As Drago slapped Eve again, Brady spotted something that

made his knees go weak with relief. Eve was lying in such a way that he could see up her skirt, and she was wearing his pistol.

And then Harry made a bunch of reports in quick succession.

"Annika is in sight."

"Thirty seconds until the cloud cover lifts."

"Team Two is good to go."

"Team One is a go."

"Stand by."

Brady tried to relax into the state of calm readiness critical to his work. But it refused to come. He clutched his weapon until his fingers cramped and actually caught himself praying.

Drago snarled something that had Eve cringing back away from the guy on the bed. She looked utterly terrified. *Focus, dammit.* It would be over in a few seconds.

She scrambled off the bed and headed for the oceanside veranda. Drago leaped after her, snagging her around the waist. Her mouth formed a single word.

Brady.

Oh, God. He could almost hear her silent plea for him to rescue her. It was as if she was looking out here, hoping to see him, hoping against hope that he would materialize and save her.

"Green light," Harry announced.

All hell broke loose. Team One burst out of the jungle on the other side of the house to break down the front door, and somewhere in the trees, Team Two moved in to jump Annika and her boys.

A piercing alarm shattered the night. The bedroom door burst open, and Brady's eyes went wide as both bodyguards leaped into the room and slammed the door shut behind them. The bodyguards must have set up some kind of motion sensors that Team One hadn't spotted.

Not good, not good, not good. With Drago alone in the room, Brady could take the bastard out before the guy could hurt Eve. But with three heavily armed men in there, she was dead. One of them would put a bullet in her head any second.

And the moment the villa's front door slammed open, she would be dead.

The moon slid out from behind the clouds, and his only route to Eve was suddenly daylight bright. His dark clothing would show up against the white sand like a beacon.

Must save Eve.

He didn't stop to think. Didn't question his motives. He just followed his instinct and stepped out into full sight in the middle of the beach. Please God, let Eve remember the signal.

He reached for his left ear and tugged it—the signal they'd used that night in George Town when she'd pretended to shoot him for her to take the shot.

Her only chance at living through the next few seconds was to convince Drago and his men that she was on their side. That she wasn't a plant. That she wasn't bait in the trap springing around them. And to do that, she would have to shoot him.

C'mon, Eve. Do it.

He watched in slow motion terror as the sound of a wood panel smashing to smithereens ripped thought the night. Drago and the bodyguards reached for concealed weapons under their suit coats. Eve frowned.

He tugged his ear again, frantically.

Too slowly, she reached for the hem of her dress.

Gunfire erupted. Wood chips flew off the bedroom walls, and Drago and his men ducked. Drago turned toward the veranda and shouted a warning. The bastard had spotted him.

Behind Drago, Brady's pistol appeared in Eve's hand, lifting toward the beach. The guards spun to face the new threat. Spotted her weapon. Their own weapons swung up to take aim at her.

And then she nodded once at Brady over the barrel of the weapon and fired.

Chapter 15

Drago lurched in front of her as she fired over his shoulder. "What the hell—" It was all he got out before he dropped like a stone in front of her. A barrage of lead flew around her, several of the rounds passing so close to her that she felt her hair lift at their passage. She even felt something warm caress her cheek.

She spun as the bedroom door literally blew up, knocking her backward. The bodyguards, although shot to heck, were still standing. But by the time the smoke cleared, they were bullet-riddled lumps on the floor.

A soldier, so heavily armed and armored he hardly looked human, rushed forward to grab her by the arm. Without speaking, he dragged her out of the room at a dead run. The guy slowed at the front door only long enough to pull a black cloth bag over her head.

She jolted in alarm. No one had said anything about a bag over her head!

Her arms were yanked behind her back and something thin and hard went around her wrists. It pulled painfully tight. Her feet swung out from underneath her and hard, strong arms carried her at a run like a giant sack of potatoes.

"Where's Brady?" she cried. "What's going on?"

"Be quiet," someone ordered harshly.

"Is he alive? Did I kill him?"

"Be quiet, or we'll drug you," someone else threatened.

What on earth was happening to her? And what had happened to Brady? He'd dropped like a rock when she pulled the trigger. It was a thousand times worse than the first time she'd shot him, though, because this time she'd sent deadly lead into the man she loved. And it wasn't like she was any kind of expert shot who could intentionally avoid vital organ. For all she knew, she'd blown his head off or hit him directly in the heart. With her luck, she'd score a kill shot the one time in her life she absolutely had to miss the target.

She gasped when her captors swung her through space and then released her onto something hard and metal and bumpy. She slammed into something soft and someone nearby grunted.

"Annika?" she whispered.

"Shut up," Annika whispered back.

Had Brady reneged on their deal? Was she being arrested as part of Annika's gang? Had he set her up? Had he signaled her to shoot at him to frame her as a member of the terrorist cell? Afraid like she'd never been afraid in her entire life, Eve lay there quivering in shock and terror as the van lurched into motion.

She didn't know how long they drove, but a door opened nearby, and she was hauled to her feet and hustled indoors. It sounded from the shuffling around her like Annika and all three of her associates were under arrest, as well.

Eve was shoved forward, and the plastic cuffs jerked

briefly. They fell away and she flexed her cramping arms carefully. What sounded like a heavy, steel door slammed shut behind her. She stood still as silence settled around her.

"Hello? Is anyone there?" she tried.

No answer.

Cautiously, she reached for the bottom of her hood and loosened the drawstrings. No one objected. She lifted the cloth and squinted into bright, fluorescent light. She was in a prison cell. The floor was concrete, the walls cinder block. A stainless steel toilet squatted in the corner, and a concrete shelf that apparently served as both chair and bed lined the far wall. Shell-shocked, she sank onto the bench.

How long she sat there with silent tears running down her cheeks, she had no idea. Brady was gone, possibly dead. He'd betrayed her. Set her up. She was under arrest as a terrorist. Brady's superiors had all the evidence in the world to tie her to the gang. Who would ever believe her if she tried to explain that Brady had signaled her to shoot him?

Her life was over. But without Brady, she couldn't drum up enough energy to care. She laid down on the cold, hard bench and died inside.

Perhaps an hour passed. And then, without warning, the door to her cell opened. A big, stern-looking man she'd never seen before gestured for her to put the bag back on. All the life drained out of her, she pulled the black sack on.

The man took her by the elbow and led her out. They walked for several minutes. A door opened, and Eve smelled the ocean, felt muggy air on her skin. They were going outdoors. Maybe if she was lucky, they'd stand her in front of a firing squad and put her out of her misery. The man helped her into a vehicle, a minivan by the height of the door and the seats. He buckled her seat belt across her, and the door slid shut beside her.

Eve jolted violently as a familiar female voice spoke beside her. *Jennifer.* "Hang in with the charade for just a little longer, Eve. This is all for your protection."

"What is going on?" Eve demanded.

"We had to arrest you along with Annika and her boys to make them think you were one of them. If you got special treatment, they'd know you were an infiltrator."

She sat upright abruptly. "Brady. Is he okay?"

"I'm taking you to him now."

Oh, no. Jennifer didn't answer the question. "Is he alive? Did I accidentally kill him?"

"He's alive," Jennifer replied tightly.

But not much more, apparently. "Can I see him? Please. It's urgent that I talk to him. Explain…"

"All in good time," was Jennifer's only reply.

The van stopped at what sounded and felt like near the ocean. Eve was escorted down a wooden pier and into a boat of some kind. Powerful engines roared, and the boat pulled away from shore at high speed if the way the hood plastered to her face was any indication. She was surprised when Jennifer explained gently that Eve had to continue to wear the hood for a while longer. Apparently, their destination was some big secret, and Eve wasn't allowed to see where they were going.

They bumped across the ocean in the speedboat for several hours before the engines finally powered down.

And then Jennifer spoke again. "Almost there."

Eve stumbled along as she was led into what felt like some sort of small building. And then she was led into… an elevator. The floor lurched and they began to descend. The door opened, and Jennifer guided her out. Eve heard the soft swish of the door closing behind them, and then the hood lifted away from her head. A stone tunnel of some kind stretched away in front of them.

"Come with me," Jennifer ordered briskly.

They passed a number of unmarked doors and turned a few times. Eve was thoroughly lost before they finally stopped in front of another unmarked door. Jennifer reached for the handle and opened the door, gesturing for Eve to enter.

"You're not coming in with me?" Eve asked nervously.

"It's not another jail cell. I promise."

Eve stepped inside. And stopped dead in her tracks. It was as if she'd walked into a nicely furnished condo, but without any windows. A movement across the room caught her attention, and Eve sobbed aloud. She flung herself forward and into Brady's arms.

"You're alive! Thank God."

He made a pained sound as she slammed into him.

"Are you hurt? Did I shoot you?"

"You winged my left side. No serious damage. It was a great shot, actually."

"I'm never shooting another gun again as long as I live," she declared in abject relief. She stepped back far enough to look at him, and her hands couldn't seem to stop running over his chest, searching for further injuries.

"Are you sorry you didn't kill me?" he asked soberly.

"Are you crazy? I've been out of my mind with panic that I hurt you or worse." An awkward silence built between them as they stared at one another. So much hung between them, unsaid, she hardly knew where to begin.

Finally, she asked, "Why did you do it?"

"Do what?"

"Signal me to shoot you?"

"To save your life. If Drago and his guards decided you were part of the sting operation to bag them, they'd have killed you on the spot. With three armed men in there, I couldn't have shot them all before one of them turned his weapon on you. Thank God you took the shot."

He wrapped his arms around her. His embrace was careful in deference to his bandaged side, but it still felt like pure heaven.

"Brady, I love you."

His head whipped up and he went utterly still against her. "I beg your pardon?"

"I love you."

"When did you figure that out? I thought you hated my guts."

She sighed. "Didn't you know love and hate are the flip sides of the same coin? I figured it out when you sent me your pistol. I knew then, that despite everything else, despite the mission, you really cared for me. I don't expect you to love me back. I know you don't think much of women in general, but—"

A finger pressed against her lips, stilling them mid-sentence. "Eve. I showed myself to a room full of armed killers and ordered you to shoot me. What in this world besides true love would cause me to do something that crazy?"

She thought about it for several seconds before lifting her stunned gaze to his worried one. "You love me?"

"Enough to sacrifice the mission, my career—hell, my life—for you."

The butterflies in her stomach took flight one last time in a glorious rush that flashed all the colors of the rainbow in an iridescently joyous cloud.

"But we got Annika, right?" Eve asked.

"And her men. They're all in custody. Her brother and his men are dead, and his customer is in custody. Not only did you stop a dangerous terrorist cell, you stopped a major arms dealer while you were at it."

Eve smiled up at him in dawning relief. "Then it's over? Really over?"

"The mission may be over," he answered carefully, "but I'm hoping with all my heart and soul that you and I are not over."

The butterflies burst out of her and she wrapped her arms around his neck, laughing aloud with joy. She whispered through the tears obscuring her vision, "We're not over, Brady. We're just beginning."

"Marry me."

"I thought you'd never ask."

"Is that a yes?"

"Of course it is, you beautiful, wonderful man."

Laughing with her, he lifted her off the floor and swung her around, despite his wound. And then he kissed her, and she kissed him back. The future—their future—took shape before them then, a long and happy journey together, their own happily ever after all tied up with a bow and just waiting for them to unwrap it.

* * * * *

Harlequin®

ROMANTIC
SUSPENSE

COMING NEXT MONTH

Available July 26, 2011

#1667 DOUBLE DECEPTION
Code Name: Danger
Merline Lovelace

#1668 SPECIAL OPS BODYGUARD
The Kelley Legacy
Beth Cornelison

#1669 COLD CASE REUNION
Native Country
Kimberly Van Meter

#1670 BEST MAN FOR THE JOB
Meredith Fletcher

You can find more information on upcoming
Harlequin® titles, free excerpts and more at
www.HarlequinInsideRomance.com.

REQUEST YOUR FREE BOOKS!
2 FREE NOVELS PLUS 2 FREE GIFTS!

ROMANTIC
SUSPENSE
Sparked by Danger, Fueled by Passion.

YES! Please send me 2 FREE Harlequin® Romantic Suspense novels and my 2 FREE gifts (gifts are worth about $10). After receiving them, if I don't wish to receive any more books, I can return the shipping statement marked "cancel." If I don't cancel, I will receive 4 brand-new novels every month and be billed just $4.49 per book in the U.S. or $5.24 per book in Canada. That's a saving of at least 14% off the cover price! It's quite a bargain! Shipping and handling is just 50¢ per book in the U.S. and 75¢ per book in Canada.* I understand that accepting the 2 free books and gifts places me under no obligation to buy anything. I can always return a shipment and cancel at any time. Even if I never buy another book, the two free books and gifts are mine to keep forever.

240/340 HDN FEFR

Name	(PLEASE PRINT)	
Address		Apt. #
City	State/Prov.	Zip/Postal Code

Signature (if under 18, a parent or guardian must sign)

Mail to the **Reader Service:**
IN U.S.A.: P.O. Box 1867, Buffalo, NY 14240-1867
IN CANADA: P.O. Box 609, Fort Erie, Ontario L2A 5X3

Not valid for current subscribers to Harlequin Romantic Suspense books.

**Want to try two free books from another line?
Call 1-800-873-8635 or visit www.ReaderService.com.**

* Terms and prices subject to change without notice. Prices do not include applicable taxes. Sales tax applicable in N.Y. Canadian residents will be charged applicable taxes. Offer not valid in Quebec. This offer is limited to one order per household. All orders subject to credit approval. Credit or debit balances in a customer's account(s) may be offset by any other outstanding balance owed by or to the customer. Please allow 4 to 6 weeks for delivery. Offer available while quantities last.

Your Privacy—The Reader Service is committed to protecting your privacy. Our Privacy Policy is available online at www.ReaderService.com or upon request from the Reader Service.

We make a portion of our mailing list available to reputable third parties that offer products we believe may interest you. If you prefer that we not exchange your name with third parties, or if you wish to clarify or modify your communication preferences, please visit us at www.ReaderService.com/consumerschoice or write to us at Reader Service Preference Service, P.O. Box 9062, Buffalo, NY 14269. Include your complete name and address.

HRS11B

*Once bitten, twice shy. That's Gabby Wade's motto—
especially when it comes to Adamson men.
And the moment she meets Jon Adamson her theory
is confirmed. But with each encounter a little something
sparks between them, making her wonder if she's been
too hasty to dismiss this one!*

*Enjoy this sneak peek from ONE GOOD REASON
by Sarah Mayberry, available August 2011
from Harlequin® Superromance®.*

Gabby Wade's heartbeat thumped in her ears as she marched to her office. She wanted to pretend it was because of her brisk pace returning from the file room, but she wasn't that good a liar.

Her heart was beating like a tom-tom because Jon Adamson had touched her. In a very male, very possessive way. She could still feel the heat of his big hand burning through the seat of her khakis as he'd steadied her on the ladder.

It had taken every ounce of self-control to tell him to unhand her. What she'd really wanted was to grab him by his shirt and, well, explore all those urges his touch had instantly brought to life.

While she might not like him, she was wise enough to understand that it wasn't always about liking the other person. Sometimes it was about pure animal attraction.

Refusing to think about it, she turned to work. When she'd typed in the wrong figures three times, Gabby admitted she was too tired and too distracted. Time to call it a day.

As she was leaving, she spied Jon at his workbench in the shop. His head was propped on his hand as he studied blueprints. It wasn't until she got closer that she saw his eyes were shut.

He looked oddly boyish. There was something innocent and unguarded in his expression. She felt a weakening in her resistance to him.

"Jon." She put her hand on his shoulder, intending to shake him awake. Instead, it rested there like a caress.

His eyes snapped open.

"You were asleep."

"No, I was, uh, visualizing something on this design." He gestured to the blueprint in front of him then rubbed his eyes.

That gesture dealt a bigger blow to her resistance. She realized it wasn't only animal attraction pulling them together. She took a step backward as if to get away from the knowledge.

She cleared her throat. "I'm heading off now."

He gave her a smile, and she could see his exhaustion.

"Yeah, I should, too." He stood and stretched. The hem of his T-shirt rose as he arched his back and she caught a flash of hard male belly. She looked away, but it was too late. Her mind had committed the image to permanent memory.

And suddenly she knew, for good or bad, she'd never look at Jon the same way again.

Find out what happens next in ONE GOOD REASON, available August 2011 from Harlequin® Superromance®!

Celebrating

Blaze™ **10** *years of*
red-hot reads

Featuring a special August author lineup of
six fan-favorite authors who have written
for Blaze™ from the beginning!

The Original Sexy Six:

Vicki Lewis Thompson
Tori Carrington
Kimberly Raye
Debbi Rawlins
Julie Leto
Jo Leigh

Pick up all six Blaze™
Special Collectors' Edition titles!

August 2011

Plus visit
HarlequinInsideRomance.com
and click on the Series Excitement Tab
for exclusive Blaze™ 10th Anniversary content!

USA TODAY *bestselling author*

Lynne Graham

introduces her new Epic Duet

THE VOLAKIS VOW

A marriage made of secrets…

Tally Spencer, an ordinary girl with no experience of
relationships… Sander Volakis, an impossibly rich and
handsome Greek entrepreneur. Sander is expecting to
love her and leave her, but for Tally this is love at first
sight. Little does he know that Tally is expecting his
baby…and blackmailing him to marry her!

PART ONE:
THE MARRIAGE BETRAYAL
Available August 2011

PART TWO:
BRIDE FOR REAL
Available September 2011

Available only from Harlequin Presents®.

INTRIGUE

USA TODAY BESTSELLING AUTHOR

B.J. DANIELS

**BRINGS READERS
THE NEXT INSTALLMENT IN
THE SUSPENSEFUL MINISERIES**

WHITEHORSE MONTANA

Chisholm Cattle Company

Alexa Cross has returned to the old Wellington Manor that her brother believes is haunted to prove to him that she is not psychic, as their mother was. Although she soon realizes that the trouble isn't with spirits but instead is all too human.

Alexa finds herself running for her life—straight into neighboring rancher Marshall Chisholm's arms. Marshall doesn't believe the old mansion is haunted. But he does believe Alexa is in serious trouble if she stays there.

Can Marshall help keep Alexa safe from a possible killer?
Find out in:

STAMPEDED

Available August 2011 from Harlequin Intrigue

3 more titles to follow…
Available wherever books are sold.

SPECIAL EDITION

Life, Love, Family and Top Authors!

IN AUGUST, HARLEQUIN SPECIAL EDITION FEATURES
USA TODAY BESTSELLING AUTHORS
MARIE FERRARELLA AND *ALLISON LEIGH.*

THE BABY WORE A BADGE
BY *MARIE FERRARELLA*

The second title in the **Montana Mavericks:
The Texans Are Coming!** miniseries....

Suddenly single father Jake Castro has his hands full with
the baby he never expected—and with a beautiful young
woman too wise for her years.

COURTNEY'S BABY PLAN
BY *ALLISON LEIGH*

The third title in the **Return to the Double C** miniseries....

Tired of waiting for Mr. Right, nurse Courtney Clay takes
matters into her own hands to create the family she's
always wanted— but her surly patient may just be
the Mr. Right she's been searching for all along.

**Look for these titles and others in August 2011
from Harlequin Special Edition wherever books are sold.**

BIG SKY BRIDE, BE MINE! *(Northridge Nuptials)* by *VICTORIA PADE*
THE MOMMY MIRACLE by *LILIAN DARCY*
THE MOGUL'S MAYBE MARRIAGE by *MINDY KLASKY*
LIAM'S PERFECT WOMAN by *BETH KERY*
